"How'd you get that scar?"

"Some people might call that question nosy." He towered over her desk.

Marly refused to be intimidated. "Some people might not be trying to protect themselves."

He cocked his head to one side. "From me?"

"If necessary. Is it necessary, Sam?"

His smile was lethal. No doubt she was going to dream about those dark brown eyes.

"Nope. But I assume your bedroom door has a lock?"

The question shocked her. That was probably exactly what he intended, she realized. "You're trying to distract me."

He regarded her with a naughty expression that sent inexplicable tingles of excitement singing through her body. "Is it working?" he asked.

Dear Reader,

They're rugged, they're strong and they're *wanted!* Whether sheriff, undercover cop or officer of the court, these men are trained to keep the peace, to uphold the law. But what happens when they meet the one woman who gets to know the man *behind* the badge?

Twelve of these men are on the loose...and only Harlequin Intrigue brings them to you—one per month in the LAWMAN series. This month meet cop-on-the-run Sam Moore in *Man Without a Badge,* by relative newcomer Dani Sinclair.

More than twenty-nine years ago Dani promised her fiancé their lives would never be dull. He claims she's kept her promise. Five years ago her sister caught Dani between career moves and demanded she finally write a book. Dani isn't sure this is how careers are supposed to be born, but she's delighted to throw all the blame on her sister. Dani lives with her husband and two grown sons in a small suburb in Maryland outside Washington, D.C. *Man Without a Badge* is Dani's second Harlequin Intrigue novel.

"Take a sizzling attraction, sprinkle it with humor and add a dash of mystery. That's my idea of cooking."

Good thing her family likes to eat out.

Be sure you don't miss Sam's exciting story—or any of the LAWMAN books coming to you in the months ahead...because there's nothing sexier than the strong arms of the law!

Regards,

Debra Matteucci
Senior Editor and Editorial Coordinator
Harlequin Books
300 East 42nd Street
New York, New York 10017

Man Without a Badge
Dani Sinclair

Harlequin Books

TORONTO • NEW YORK • LONDON
AMSTERDAM • PARIS • SYDNEY • HAMBURG
STOCKHOLM • ATHENS • TOKYO • MILAN
MADRID • WARSAW • BUDAPEST • AUCKLAND

To three special ladies: Cynthia C. Parker, Courtney Henke and Laura DeVries who helped in special ways. And always, for Roger, Chip, Dan and Barb with love.

Acknowledgments
Jim Tremé and the staff of the Blue Ridge Arsenal in Virginia, for their patience with my many questions.

ISBN 0-373-22401-X

MAN WITHOUT A BADGE

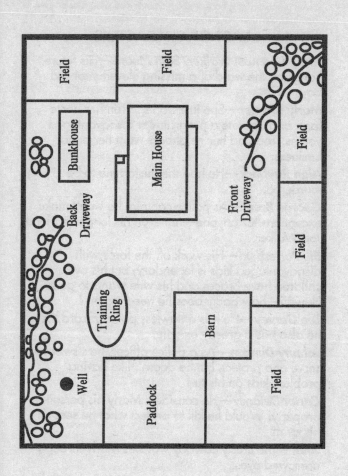

Field

Field

Field

Bunkhouse

Main House

Field

Back Driveway

Front Driveway

Field

Training Ring

Well

Barn

Paddock

Field

CAST OF CHARACTERS

Joseph Samuel Walker/Sam Moore—His future hangs on the word of a missing eleven-year-old boy.

Marly Kramer—She just wants to run her horse farm and operate a program for disadvantaged youths. Too bad her neighbors want her out of business.

Alan Rayback—He had the misfortune to be murdered.

George Brent—As police captain, he won't make exceptions for anyone—not even his longtime friend Joe Walker.

Bill Porterfield—His work off the force with disadvantaged kids is legendary, but his own children have braces and his wife wants to go to Hawaii—how badly does he need money?

Lee Garvey—He has a flawless police record, but he also has a greedy ex-wife.

Johnny Duncan—As a police officer, he's sworn to serve and protect, but he doesn't like having problem kids on his turf.

Carter Delancy—He considers Marly his personal property. Would he kill to protect what he sees as his own?

Jake—The crusty cowboy watches Marly through narrowed eyes.

Emma—There isn't much that gets by this housekeeper's watchful eyes.

The kids—Chris, Donald, Hector, Jerome, Mickey and Zeke. One of them holds the key to Joe's future.

Prologue

Fear sat like an uninvited guest, isolating the small corner table from the rest of the noisy bar.

"I'm telling you, internal affairs will be crawling all over us first thing in the morning." Porterfield stared at the glum faces surrounding him.

Joe shut his eyes, picked up his glass and drained the contents. He blotted his carefully tended mustache with the paper napkin and laid it on the table. The beer, warm now, sat heavily on his abused stomach. Automatically he opened his eyes and reached into his tailored shirt pocket for the ever-present roll of antacid tablets.

Lee slammed down his empty glass, and his handsome face turned ugly with the ferocity of his scowl. A litany of invective rolled past his lips.

"Take it easy," Joe advised.

Porterfield used two fingers to massage his temple. "I shouldn't have said anything."

Silvers sighed and reached for a handful of pretzels. "What difference does it make, man? We'd all know about it come morning."

"Why are they after us?" Lee demanded. "We had probable cause, and enough evidence to bring Rayback down. The bust was textbook."

Porterfield shook his head, his spectacles reflecting the neon light over the bar. "*Had* is the operative word. Somebody got into the evidence room. The money's gone."

Joe's stomach tightened another notch. "What do you mean, somebody?"

Porterfield stopped rubbing his temple. "Five of us signed in."

Silvers swallowed a pretzel. "Who's the fifth?"

"The captain."

The two words hung suspended in the air, alongside the fear. The four men slid glances around the room, trying not to stare at one another.

"That's nuts," Lee said suddenly. "We work our tails off to make this bust stick and they think one of us stole the evidence?"

"Fifty thousand in cash is a lot of money," Joe said quietly.

"You confessing?" Porterfield asked with a droll grin.

"Nope. I'm just saying if the money is missing, the captain had no choice but to call Internal Affairs."

"Did you know about it, Joe?" Lee asked.

Joe shook his head. "He and I may be friends, but you know the captain. No preferential treatment. He always plays by the rules."

"Maybe the captain took it. Maybe he needed money for those old cars he's always fixing up."

"Yeah. He's been actin' like a bear with a sore paw for weeks lately. Must be woman trouble." Silvers grabbed another handful of pretzels. "That wife of his is some kinda looker."

"Knock it off," Lee rebuked.

Porterfield grinned. "Well, I only hope he shares the

wealth with us poor working stiffs. I've got two kids in braces and a wife who wants to vacation in Hawaii.''

"It isn't one of us,'' Silvers stated. He pushed back his chair and stood. ''I gotta get home or LaTisha will skin my sorry hide. We got nothin' to hide an' nothin' to fear.''

Maybe so, but Joe knew they were all scared. Careers were at stake here. Word would get out. IA would put them under a microscope, and suddenly four good cops would start looking at one another with suspicion instead of trust.

''Damn.''

''Yeah.'' Lee nodded. ''Want to go get a bite to eat?''

Joe shook his head. He didn't want company. He needed to work off this new frustration. ''I think I'll head over to the gym for a while.''

Bill Porterfield stood and patted his pudgy stomach. ''Do a few sit-ups for me while you're at it, will you? The wife just started me on a new diet, and I'm hating life.''

The other three smiled. Bill and his wife's diets were legendary. Tonight, the diets provided a welcome source of humor as the men parted company in the parking lot.

Two hours later, Joe was still tense, but now he was also hot, sweaty and hungry. He took a quick shower, trying to pull his thoughts away from Porterfield's revelation. As he dressed, he chatted with two of the guys from vice who were just coming in. Tomorrow, word would spread. Tomorrow, these same two men would give him a wide berth out of fear for their own careers, and it would stay that way until the investigation was concluded. Distracted, Joe snapped his small holster into place, reached for his jacket and fumbled for his keys. Food no longer held any appeal.

The city streets were still damp and slick from the earlier rain. He ignored the lit monuments as he drove past them, scanning the empty sidewalks out of habit. An accident had blocked the ramp leading to the Beltway, so he decided to take the scenic route through Rock Creek Park. A rumble of thunder added the perfect touch. More rain. It suited his mood.

Because he wasn't really looking for anything, he went past the parked car before its distinctive license plate registered in the back of his mind.

RAYBACK.

Only Rayback was under lock and key. How had he gotten sprung so fast? And what the hell was he doing in Rock Creek Park at this hour? It took Joe a quarter of a mile to find a spot to turn around.

He lifted the car phone, then hesitated. The threat of IA was making him paranoid. He knew he should call for backup, but he replaced the phone in its holder.

Backup because Rayback is taking a walk in a public park?

No, backup because whatever Rayback was doing in this park, a few miles from the police station, would have nothing to do with walking and probably everything to do with the reason IA was coming in the morning.

Joe pulled in alongside the other car. It was locked and empty. Even as he called himself ten kinds of fool, he was headed down the path, unbuttoning his jacket as he went.

The indistinct sound of angry voices soon slowed his pace as another warning rumble of thunder sounded overhead. The same darkness that provided protection for him would offer concealment for Rayback and anyone else in this wooded section.

Trees and shrubs parted abruptly for a narrow clearing. Only Rayback's distinctive white hair made it possible to spot him at all. Joe couldn't make out the other person, deep in the shadows of a large pine tree. He edged closer. As he pulled his gun free of its holster, he stopped in utter shock. It wasn't his gun.

What the hell?

A twig snapped to his left. He brought the semiautomatic in line with the sound, pulled back the slide, and just barely stopped himself from squeezing the trigger. A pair of wide, serious eyes stared back at him. The kid couldn't have been more than eleven or twelve.

"Don't shoot me, mister!"

Three shots rang out in quick succession.

Joe spun, to see Rayback crumpling to the ground.

"Police! Freeze!"

Even as the words left his lips, Joe knew it was too late. The gunman had heard the boy cry out. His weapon spit another stream of fire. Joe squeezed his own trigger and belatedly realized there was no cartridge in the clip.

Thunder exploded in his ear. White-hot pain took him to the cold, damp ground. His last conscious thought was that he hoped the boy had run.

Chapter One

Sunlight glinted off the blade of the knife. The boy went into a crouch and circled his opponent.

"Jerome, put that down this minute. You won't settle anything like this." Tension choked Marly's voice. Jerome didn't spare her a glance. His eleven-year-old eyes stayed fixed on the other boy.

"Mickey, tell him where his watch is." Real fear pierced her, much sharper than the blade of the knife her charge was holding. It was a good bet Jerome hadn't heard her words. For certain he wasn't going to obey them. She was going to have to take the knife away from him herself.

"You're holdin' it all wrong, kid."

The soft drawl sliced across the scene, freezing everyone in the noonday sun. Marly lifted her head in surprise to see a stranger lounging against the fender of her pickup truck. Not just any stranger. Every woman's fantasy cowboy, come to life. From his scuffed boots to his formfitting work jeans to the denim jacket and the chambray work shirt open at the neck, he exuded a masculine strength that trapped her breath in her throat. A dusty duffel bag sat on the ground at his feet, and a black cowboy hat was pulled low over his brow.

He used his index finger to push the brim upward a notch as he came off the fender in a fluid movement that riveted her senses. Suddenly, a wicked blade gleamed in his hand, as well.

Mickey and Jerome turned to stone, fixated on the deadly knife in the stranger's hand. Marly wanted to swallow, but her tight throat wouldn't oblige her.

There was an aura of quiet danger about the man. Unlike Jerome, he held his knife as if he knew what to do with it and had done it often.

"You pull a knife on someone, you'd better know how to use it, kid. Pull your arm in closer to your body, like this." He went into a menacing crouch.

From somewhere, Marly found her voice. Quaking with fright, she placed herself between the stranger and her boys. "Put that away." Amazingly, the command came out firm and controlled. She refused to let him see her fear, but its metallic taste filled her mouth.

The knife disappeared in a blur of motion, and the stranger stood erect. "Yes, ma'am. Didn't mean to scare you." His easy drawl sent goose bumps up and down her arms. His glance moved past her, to the two boys at her back. "Seems to me if a man's gonna pull a weapon, he'd better be prepared for the consequences."

His long stride placed him within touching distance. Putting away the knife had done nothing to diminish her sense of danger. If anything, it was now more acute than ever. She could scream, but help was too far away. Still, she needed to protect the boys.

He watched her in silence. There was a day's growth of beard on that firm jaw and, looking up, she saw that his eyes were brown. A dark liquid brown, warm and safe.

Safe? Marly shook her head at the bizarre notion and

the spell was broken. The stranger stepped around her and placed a hand on Jerome's thin, bony arm still holding the small blade.

"In against your body like this," he told the boy, positioning the arm. "That way, your opponent can't come in under you. You ever knife somebody, kid?"

Wide eyes stared up at the stranger with a mixture of awe and fear. Slowly the boy's wiry head moved from side to side.

"Didn't think so." The man rested a gentle hand on Jerome's shoulder. "It isn't pretty what a knife can do. Messy, too. Knife wounds bleed like hell."

Marly was sure his words came from experience.

His head tipped toward Mickey. "You figure bein' scarred for life is worth a watch, kid?"

Mickey's twelve-year-old head lifted defiantly, but Marly saw the fear in his clear blue eyes. "I ain't scared."

"Then you're a fool."

"I don't got his damn watch."

"Mickey!" Marly exclaimed. The situation was spiraling out of control. The stranger was making it worse. She could have handled things if he hadn't interrupted.

"Well, I don't," Mickey insisted, his eyes fixed on the stranger. "The squirt here set it up there on the railing this morning." Mickey nodded toward the porch that wrapped around two-thirds of the old farmhouse.

Jerome started toward the porch, but Marly scooted in front of him and held out her hand. "The knife."

Rebellious eyes met hers. He gave his head a quick shake. "No way, man."

Her words of admonishment went unspoken as that soft drawl took over.

"That's two more things you'd better learn, kid.

When to obey a direct order, and how to treat a lady. The first will make life easier. The second will make life real enjoyable. She's a ma'am, not a man."

Frissons of awareness skated through her body at his husky words. There was no mistaking his meaning about life being enjoyable. Marly straightened, aware of his gaze on the thrust of her breasts against her plaid shirt. Before she could think of a reply, he turned back to Jerome.

"Give her the knife, kid. Later on, I'll show you a better use for it."

"Now just a min—"

"It's mine," Jerome told them defiantly.

"Nobody's disputin' it, kid. But the lady's in control right now. You'll get it back." He tossed her a measuring look. "Won't he?"

Marly blinked. She could almost hear his silent command to back him up. "Yes, of course. But—"

"See there?"

Long seconds crawled by. Reluctantly Jerome closed the blade and laid it in her palm. He started to turn away, but the stranger's voice nailed him again. "I think you owe your adversary an apology."

Jerome shook his head. "Not till I find my watch."

The stranger's lips lifted at the corner. He tipped his head in acknowledgment. "Fair enough."

"I'll show you where you left it," Mickey said suddenly.

The two boys eyed one another before Jerome nodded and the taller, beefier Mickey turned and headed for the front porch. Marly spun to face the big man before the boys were even out of hearing distance. "Just who do you think you are?"

"Your new hand."

He had hands, all right. Large, work-roughened hands. Hands that looked very capable of doing just about anything, from lifting a bale of hay to holding a woman.

"I didn't hire any new hands," she said, trying to shake that last crazy image.

"Yet."

The word hung in the silence as they surveyed one another. Marly chewed on her lower lip, and his gaze fastened on her mouth, making her aware again of her isolated status. "I don't thi—"

"You advertised for someone who knew horses and kids. The ad said room and board went with the deal."

Her immediate response was to deny it, but she couldn't afford to turn away any offer of help right now. She was already woefully short-staffed, and with all the accidents lately...

"What do you know about horses?"

"Which end to feed and which end not to walk behind."

"That isn't very reassuring."

His lips twisted upward the slightest bit. "You've already seen I can handle kids. Want me to show you what else I can do?"

Blood thrummed in her ears, momentarily drowning out any other sound. She could think of any number of things she'd bet he did well, and not one of them had to do with horses.

"I'll need references," she managed to say.

The curl of amusement stayed in place around his lips. A drift of heat moved upward to settle on her cheeks. He couldn't possibly know what she'd just been thinking.

"No problem."

Ha! Easy for him to say. This man was already a big problem. Look what he was doing to her hormone levels. She smoothed her hands down the sides of her dusty jeans, and he followed the movement with his eyes. "The job doesn't pay all that much," she added quickly.

"Good thing I don't need all that much, then, isn't it?"

No answering retort sprang to mind. At least not one that couldn't be interpreted in ways she didn't want to contemplate. "Do you have a name?"

"Sam."

Marly braced her hands on her hips and decided it was long past time to take the initiative. This was her horse farm, her camp, and he'd be one of her hired hands—if she hired him. She assumed an assertive posture, hoping she looked in control. "Look, mister, I don't have time to play twenty questions. I get the impression you aren't all that serious about this job."

His broad shoulders seemed to expand, stretching the denim of his jacket to impressive lengths. "On the contrary, ma'am, I'm as serious as anyone you'll ever meet."

His words encircled her. She believed him. There was an intensity to his voice that hadn't been there before, and that subtle hint of a smile was gone. Also, his drawl was less pronounced.

The last bit was interesting, and faintly disturbing.

"The name's Samuel Moore. I've worked horse ranches from one coast to the other. My last job was working for a couple who breed show horses. Allie and Greg Norton. They've got three kids, and I helped with them, as well."

"Helped how?"

His humor returned. She could see it in the twinkle

of his dark eyes and the way his body relaxed into its former easy stance. "I taught the youngest how to sit a horse, the oldest how to take a water hurdle, and the middle one how to defend herself from the other two. Her brothers tend to be bossy." He sounded like a proud father.

"I trust you didn't resort to knives?"

That elicited a half smile and a nod of acknowledgment of the way he had handled the earlier situation. "Nope. Where her brothers were concerned, I suggested clubs."

She had to hold back an urge to smile at him. "How reassuring."

"I can give you a number to call."

Damn. She liked this stranger, and not just for his looks, which were pretty spectacular, by any woman's standards. More importantly, he had a droll sense of humor, and she liked the fact that he hadn't talked down to the boys, even when Jerome was so obviously out of control.

Maybe she should have handled that situation a bit differently, she acknowledged, but she hadn't appreciated the way he barged in and took control. Even though he'd been a help, she hadn't liked his none-too-subtle methods one bit. Still, she hesitated.

"Where are you from, cowboy?"

The touch of sarcasm in her voice didn't seem to bother him in the least.

"Utah."

"Utah's a long way from suburban Maryland, cowboy."

"Sam. You can take the phone charges out of my first week's wages."

"That isn't what I meant. What chased you out of Utah?"

"Cherry blossoms," he replied promptly.

Marly blinked, not sure she had heard him correctly. "I beg your pardon?"

"I'd never seen them. Only pictures. It happened to be the right time of year when the urge to move on struck me, so I hitched a ride this direction. They're beautiful, you know. They've got a fragile magnificence that pictures just don't capture."

Marly stared at him, perplexed. A self-proclaimed cowboy and drifter with the heart of a poet? His explanation was too bizarre not to be true, yet it was hard to imagine this man wandering in a grove of cherry blossoms. She was distracted from the thought by the sound of rapidly approaching hoofbeats.

SAM LIFTED HIS HEAD to study the bantam-size man who reigned in his horse outside the barn, hitched it to a fence and swaggered over.

"He'd better be looking for a job, Marly."

Sam tightened, not liking the man or his tone of voice.

"What's wrong now, Jake?" Marly sounded resigned.

"The new guy got thrown in the south pasture. His leg's fractured in at least two places. Stupid horse stepped on him."

"I'll get my truck."

"Don't bother. Lou and Keefer are driving him into town in the red pickup, but he won't be able to help you with the brats anymore for a while."

Marly straightened as if she were spring-loaded. She took two steps forward and faced Jake squarely. Sam could almost feel the waves of anger rolling off her.

"This is your last warning. You refer to those boys as brats or make any other derogatory comment about them again and I'll cut you your severance pay on the spot. Got it?"

His eyes narrowed to mean slits, and he took a step forward. Sam moved to stand beside Marly. He didn't say a word. He didn't have to. He knew how to project an aura of stark intimidation, and he used that knowledge, letting menace roll off him like heat from a desert rock.

Jake stopped. Surprise and calculation flittered across his pinched features.

"We got five sections of fencing down in the south pasture," he said finally, pretending to ignore Sam, "and four of your prize yearlings are running free. You got any other *orders*, boss lady?"

Marly did clench her jaw then. Sam wondered why she didn't order the insubordinate little runt off the property then and there.

"How can we have fences down? We just replaced every... Never mind. Where's Carter?"

"Playing baby-sitter to your...*boys*. He's got most of 'em over at the training corral. You want me to go get him?"

"No. You start getting those yearlings rounded up."

"By myself?"

"Take Sam with you." She tilted her head and acknowledged Sam for the first time since Jake had arrived. "You're hired, if you still want the job. I hope you know how to saddle a horse."

"Yes, ma'am. I can even stay on top of one."

Marly didn't respond to that. She pivoted and headed for the main stable, leaving the two men to follow.

"Put the yearlings in the west pasture until we get

the fences back up. Jake, show Sam where to get some tack," she added, tossing the words over her shoulder.

Ponytail swinging, she headed away from the large barn and started down the hill. "I'll let Carter know what happened." She paused, as if a thought had occurred to her. "What happened to his horse?"

"Stupid beast took off."

"Great. Just great. Get out there before those yearlings make it as far as the road. All I need is for one of my neighbors to get in a car wreck because of loose horses."

"They'd be madder if it was one of your *boys* on the loose."

"Get a move on, Jake." She took her own advice and broke into a graceful run.

Sam watched her go. She had an easy, loping stride for a woman. Her sun-bleached ponytail swung against her back in a feminine way that was strangely sensual. Marly was real easy on the eyes, Sam decided. But he didn't like the ugly way Jake watched her, as well.

"The tack room?" Sam bit out.

Jake's expression went from lustful to annoyed, to openly curious and slightly hostile.

"I don't think I caught your name, mister."

"Sam." And Sam let his long legs eat up the distance in the direction of the main stable. Jake was left with no option but to scurry along behind.

Sam would have preferred to follow Marly to the practice ring he could see in the distance. A tall man was watching a horse and rider canter, while three other youths leaned on the fence to watch.

The kids were too far away for a clear view. Sam consoled himself with the knowledge that he'd found the right place. He'd even landed a job, and she hadn't asked any questions. Luck was with him so far. He'd find the right boy. It could wait an hour or so.

Sam paused inside the barn to wait for Jake. The scent of horses hung heavy in the early-June heat. It was a far cry from the womanly scent that he'd caught a whiff of when he was standing next to Marly.

"Tack's through there." Jake eyed him thoughtfully. "I'll get Dickens for you."

Sam was going to have trouble with Jake. Particularly if the cowboy continued to look at Marly the way he had a few minutes ago. He wondered if Jake had a record anywhere. He wondered what the odds were that Jake would recognize him.

Dressed as he was now, with the hat covering most of his features and minus his mustache, Sam Moore could only hope he looked nothing like the fastidious Joseph Samuel Walker. Every cop in at least five states was looking for the renegade cop—the one wanted for murder and graft.

Sam selected his equipment and headed back outside. He was thinking it was a good thing his family had called him Sammy as a kid, so as not to confuse him with his father, Joe, and his cousin Joey. It made it easier to stay in character and think of himself as Sam instead of Joe.

He was basking in his luck when Jake led a large, fractious roan around front as he emerged. Sam hadn't been on a horse in over a year, but it didn't take a genius to guess Jake had picked the most difficult animal in the corral for him to ride. It was either a test or petty revenge. Either way, Sam was in for an exacting afternoon. He heaved a mental sigh and stepped forward.

"Jake! What the hell are you doing?"

Sam turned to see a man about his own age hurrying

toward them. It was the man from the training ring, if Sam wasn't mistaken.

"What are you doing with Dickens? You know he isn't fit for a saddle yet."

Jake's mouth pursed, and he shot Sam a hard look, as if to say this was all his fault. "Marly said I was to—"

"Never mind. The new guy can use Ginger."

"Then who's Marly gonna ride?"

"She's going to stay with the kids until we get back."

Jake's surprise was obvious. "You mean you're going with us?"

The newcomer's voice took on a hard edge. "It's my job. I'm still the foreman, Jake. Now go get Ginger, and put Dickens back before he throws a fit."

Dickens pranced restlessly, his ears and scarred flanks twitching as his eyes flicked from side to side. Jake was having trouble controlling him with the lead rein.

"I thought your job was to baby-sit," Jake muttered as he turned the large roan around.

A quick glance at the foreman told Sam he hadn't missed the words. There was a hard edge to his eyes as he watched Jake disappear. An edge that disappeared as soon as he caught Sam's look.

"I'm Carter Delancy. You must be Sam."

The handshake was firm. Rough, work-callused hands and unwinking eye contact. Sam liked that. Beneath his gray Stetson, the man had dark hair and a lean physique. He had the kind of chiseled good looks that attracted women and a commanding authority other men respected. Sam could easily picture this man in charge.

"Sam Moore."

"Pleased to meetcha. Marly says you know your way around a ranch."

"I've mucked more than a few stalls."

"Good enough." The grin was relaxed and friendly, but it faded quickly. "I see you and Jake have already gotten off on the wrong foot."

"No problem," Sam stated mildly. "What's wrong with Dickens?"

Carter's expression tightened in angry lines. "In a human we'd call it a nervous breakdown. The vet's got some fancy name for it, but basically the fool horse got himself caught on barbed wire. Tore his flank pretty good before we got him free. I wanted to destroy him, but Marly wouldn't hear of it, and she's the boss."

Sam tilted his head. "So I gather. No Mr. Marly?"

Carter pulled on a pair of leather riding gloves. "Not anymore."

His body language warned that the subject was off-limits. Sam wondered why.

"How'd the horse get caught on barbed wire?"

"That, my friend, is something I'd like to know, as well," he stated grimly.

Jake arrived with Ginger, stopping whatever else Carter might have said. Ginger was a beautiful palomino. She stood out on a farm that bred quarter horses, and she proved to be amenable, as well as beautiful. The two men waited for Sam to saddle the mare. He was damn glad there were some things a person just didn't forget how to do.

Two hours later, he was wishing the rest of his body hadn't forgotten how to ride and do physical labor. Gym workouts just weren't the same thing at all. He was going to have a hard time hiding his stiffness, but at least the yearlings were rounded up and safely settled in another pasture.

The other two men showed up in a red pickup truck a short time later. Lifting fence posts gave Sam the perfect opportunity to check over the site of the downed fence. It didn't take an experienced eye to see what had happened. Someone had backed a truck up to the fence, tied a rope to it and then driven forward. The momentum had snapped or pulled free most of the fence posts along this section.

The tire tracks did not match those on the red pickup truck.

"What are you looking at?"

Sam lifted his head and regarded Carter. The other men were working several yards away.

"Tire tracks," Sam told Carter, pointing to the two sets. "This was no accident."

"I know."

"Any reason we aren't calling in the local law?"

"Yeah. It wouldn't do any good."

Sam waited. Carter rubbed his jaw and sighed before he leaned down to lift another post from the stack on the ground.

"I guess you have the right to know, if you're going to sign on with us. We've been having a few problems lately."

Again Sam waited. Carter set the post, and Sam began to fill in around the hole.

"Some of Marly's neighbors don't take kindly to the fact that Marly opens the farm to the kids during the summer months."

"The kids have criminal records?"

"Yeah." Carter watched him closely.

"Jake doesn't seem real happy about the kids, either."

That earned Sam a frown and a quick, hard look. "Jake has his problems, but he's a good worker and he does what he's told. I see to it he stays as far from the kids as possible."

"Good thinking. Are these hard-core hoodlums we're talking about?" he asked, even though he already knew the answer.

"No, not at all. Most of the boys are from one-parent families. Inner-city kids who never get a break. The authorities think these kids can be saved—redirected, if you will."

"What do you think?"

Carter let go of the post and started back to the truck. "See Keefer over there?"

Sam looked at the gangly youth stringing wire fencing. His lanky body looked as if it still had some growing years left, but, judging by the facial hair that was trying to become a mustache, Sam figured him at about nineteen or twenty.

"Keefer came to us from a program similar to ours, for older boys. He's clean, a hard worker, and an example of what a program like ours can do for someone in need of guidance. Marly figures if it worked for him, think how much better it could work if we started with kids even younger. That's why she picked eleven-and twelve-year-olds. This is our second year in operation."

"So why are the neighbors suddenly pulling down her fences?"

Carter looked unhappy. "There were a few problems last year."

Once again, Sam waited without a word.

"The city's mutating like a virus. We've got housing

developments right down the road a ways—nervous busybodies worried about inner-city germs of evil and destruction invading their precious darlings."

"Interestin' way of puttin' things. So last year some of them were contaminated?"

"No!" Carter backed away from the sharpness of his retort. "There were minor problems. Some petty thefts that got blamed on our kids, because, of course, no one in their tax brackets raises light-fingered children."

Sam smiled, liking Carter more by the minute. "Long memories, huh?"

Carter didn't return the smile. "Last year Marly had a husband. This year she doesn't. The neighbors think without him around to keep the boys in check, they'll be free to run wild. Particularly after word got out that our counselor quit."

Sam thought about Marly and the scene this morning. She was no marshmallow, despite her slender build. She'd been ready to step between Jerome and Mickey, even though it had been obvious to him that she lacked the knowledge to get the job done without someone getting hurt. Still, she had guts, and he liked that about her. Come to think of it, there were several things he liked about her.

"What happened to the husband?"

Carter's expression grew hard and unreadable.

"They're divorced. There's one thing you'd better understand from the start, Sam. Marly's off-limits. Got it?"

"Does that include you?"

Temper flashed in Carter's eyes, but was quickly under control. He was starting to reply when there was a shout.

"Smoke!"

Sam followed the direction of the pointing finger. A wispy thread of gray drifted upward to blend with the sky. It was some distance away. About as far away as the nearest barn.

Chapter Two

Marly continued to hold the hose long after the grass fire was out, and even after someone had turned off the water. She trembled at the near miss. Who hated her this much? Which one of her neighbors wanted to see her fail badly enough to burn her out, at the risk of the kids and animals under her protection?

Or was she being paranoid? The fire could have been an accident—couldn't it?

A strong hand closed over her fingers and kindled an immediate sense of awareness. Before lifting her head, she knew who was tugging the hose from her grasp.

"You can let go now, Marly," Sam said, taking the metal sprayer from her hand.

"What happened here?" Carter demanded. His voice pulled her back to reality.

"I don't know." Marly drew a smudged hand across her bangs and shook her head. She glanced at the boys clustered nervously behind her. "Jerome ran into the kitchen and said the field was on fire."

Jerome's narrow chest puffed forward in pride, and his white teeth gleamed against his face.

Sam dropped the hose and left her side, heading toward the sodden grass in that loose, easy stride of his.

She saw that he watched Jake who prowled the charred ground.

"How did it start?" Carter demanded.

Marly shrugged, without taking her eyes from the two men. "I haven't a clue. What happened to the fences? We just replaced the old posts a few weeks ago."

Jake bent to lift something. Sam followed his movements intently. When he turned and caught her watching, he headed back in her direction.

"Accidents happen," Carter replied.

"Particularly when they have help," Sam added, joining them.

Carter shook his head, frowning heavily, but Marly focused on Sam's stony expression. Blood rushed through her with enough force to set her trembling again.

"What kind of help?" she asked Sam.

"One of the yearlings must have—"

"Someone used a truck to pull it down," Sam stated with quiet conviction.

She fought for control, nails digging into the palms of her hands. So she wasn't paranoid. That would have been too easy. "Is what Sam says true, Carter?"

"Now, Marly—"

"Don't you dare." She had to force the words past her anger. "Don't you dare lie to me. Did someone deliberately tear down the fence?" She held his eyes, refusing to let him look away.

"Well, it could have happened that way."

"Why?"

Her question hung in the air. The pickup truck roared into the yard, and her other two employees spilled out on the run. "Everything okay?" one shouted.

No one bothered to answer. Jake ambled forward, satisfaction on his narrow face. "This is why there was a fire," he stated. The obscene remains of a cigarette butt lay on his dirty, outstretched palm. "One of your br—*boys*—was smokin' again."

Relief coursed through her. At least the fire had been an accident. Sam didn't move, yet her eyes homed in on his. She couldn't read a thing in his hard expression, so she twisted to face the boys who stood clustered together in silence, eyes downcast. "Is it true? Was someone smoking?"

"We didn't see nothin'," Chris muttered.

He was often the spokesman. The other boys tended to follow his lead. Now was no different. There was a general shuffling. None of them met her gaze.

"You know the rules," she told them quietly. "This is the reason why I have a no-smoking rule. The barn could have burned. Someone could have gotten hurt."

"Why you always gotta blame us? It coulda been one of them," Chris said, gesturing at the men who were heading toward the barn.

"No. I don't hire smokers. A barn fire is a terrifying sight." Marly closed her eyes for a second. No one made a sound. It occurred to her that she hadn't asked the new man if he smoked.

"Okay," she continued slowly. "I told you at the outset, I don't make threats. Anyone caught with cigarettes will be sent home—immediately." Six pairs of eyes measured the seriousness of her words. "The guilty party knows what he did. And you all did a great job of pulling together to put the fire out."

Her eyes strayed. Sam watched her with disconcerting approval. "End of discussion," she told them.

"Don't you even want to know who did it?" Chris asked in surprise.

"Were you smoking, Chris?" she asked.

He took a step back, his head shaking from side to side. The other boys watched in silence.

"Okay, then. You want to help the men put everything away?"

The boys seized on the excuse. As they began to help clean the yard, Carter came to stand in front of her.

"We need to talk."

"Yes, we certainly do." She still wasn't ready to forgive him for lying about the fence, even if it had been due to a misplaced need to protect her. How many other times had he lied to her?

"Look, I can't be your foreman and counselor to these kids at the same time. We've got to try and find someone to take charge of the boys. There's too much real work to be done around here."

Marly bristled, but there was truth to what Carter said. Since the counselor had quit, Carter was the only one she trusted completely with the boys. Still, his patience often wore thin, and as her trainer, he had other responsibilities.

She watched Sam help Jerome coil a length of hose. The boy looked up and grinned suddenly at something Sam had said. She hadn't liked that bit with the knife earlier, even if he had captured the boys' attention and earned their respect. He'd intimidated her, as well, yet she had the strangest sensation that she could trust him.

"You're absolutely right, Carter. I'll ask Sam to take over with the kids until we can find someone qualified."

"Hey, now, wait a minute. You can't do that."

"Why not?"

"We don't know anything about Sam. For all we know, he could be a child molester."

"Look at him, Carter. Does he act like a child molester?"

"You think he'd wear a sign saying 'I'm a child molester'?"

"Point taken."

"Marly—"

"I know, Carter. I'm not stupid. I'll call his references tonight. If he checks out, we'll use him—at least temporarily. What other choice do we have?"

"Damn it, this isn't wise."

"Neither is lying to me, Carter, but we'll take that up later, too. Send Sam and his gear to the main house when you finish. I want to talk to him."

Carter laid a hand on her arm. It didn't generate an iota of the unsettling awareness that Sam's touch had ignited.

"Marly, you can't be planning to let him sleep inside. At least put him in the bunkhouse with the rest of us at night."

There was common sense behind his words. Taking a complete stranger inside the house was a risk. So what wasn't? She'd been taking risks of one kind or another for years.

She pulled free from Carter's hold, saw his momentary anger and frustration, and felt a stab of remorse. Sooner or later, she was going to have to take a firm position, where he was concerned.

"Send Sam up to the house. I want to talk to him."

"Marly—"

"Just do it, Carter." She turned on her heels and headed for the front porch. The sense that she was being watched made her look back. Carter was stalking toward the barn in a huff, but Sam was eying her from beneath the low brim of his hat. Was she about to make a huge mistake again?

No sooner did she reach the base of the wide sweeping porch than the crunch of gravel had her spinning back around. A Montgomery County police car pulled into the yard, bringing everyone to an immediate standstill. Apprehension tightened her stomach. She looked for Carter, but the only adult in plain sight was Sam. There was a curious stillness to his posture, a peculiar expression on his strong face. Resigned to facing the inevitable, Marly started back out to intercept the squad car. She knew who would be behind the wheel.

FEAR CRAMPED Sam's gut in a painful knot that activated his ulcer. He ignored the burning sensation and measured the distance to the barn. Nearby, but not close enough. He was too exposed. He looked for another place of concealment. There wasn't time. Not without drawing attention right to him.

Maybe the cop wasn't here because of him. Maybe he had come because he saw the smoke. Sam forced himself to stand his ground. Would the hat cover enough of his face? He didn't know a lot of uniformed officers in Maryland. It was unlikely this was someone he knew professionally. He caught Marly watching, but he couldn't manage a smile. Had she seen his fear? He strove to control his breathing.

Jerome stood nearby. The youth was also staring hard at the police car. Sam realized fear was something he and all six boys had in common. The youngsters watched in quiet trepidation as the cruiser rolled to a stop a few feet away.

Marly seemed to gather herself before she strode forward briskly, dusting her hands on the back of her trim-fitting jeans. "Officer Duncan. How can I help you today?"

"Marly." The man stepped from the car, and his hard gaze swept each child in turn. "These the newest boys?"

"Yes." She bit the word off and stood her ground.

"New help?" the officer asked, swinging toward Sam.

Sam forced himself to stand perfectly still under that examination. Fear dried his mouth. The officer did look slightly familiar. They had met at some time. When? Where? Would the man she called Duncan recognize Sam as a fugitive?

The urge to reach for the gun in his boot was almost as irresistible as it was stupid. Before Sam could move, much less utter a syllable, Marly gave another terse "Yes" in answer to the officer's question. She made no move to introduce the two men.

It was unbelievably difficult to stand easy under Duncan's scrutiny. Sam had faced down armed men with fewer misgivings. Of course, then he'd been fairly confident of the outcome. He knew his odds of surviving this encounter weren't good, but he wouldn't struggle if he was unmasked. Not with all these kids around.

Marly braced her hands on her waist, drawing Duncan's full attention. "What can we do for you?"

"I just thought I'd drop by and check to be sure everything was okay. Looks like you had a problem." He inclined his head in the direction of the blackened field.

"Nothing important. A minor grass fire."

"Really?"

Marly didn't reply.

"You know, some of the neighbors are uneasy, after

all the problems last year, and what with you being divorced now and everything…''

"Thank you, Officer. Your kindness knows no bounds, does it?"

The total absence of inflection was chilling. More telling than outright anger. Duncan shifted a bit, as if he weren't sure how to reply.

A clanging noise shattered the moment. An older woman stood on the wide porch, ringing the heavy metal triangle that hung near the front steps.

"You'll have to excuse me," Marly said. "That's Emma's way of telling me I'm wanted on the telephone. Sam, you'll get the boys inside? Dinner should be ready shortly."

Marly didn't wait for an answer. She turned with regal pride and strode unhurriedly toward the house. They had been dismissed. It was brilliantly, perfectly executed.

"All right, you heard the boss," Sam drawled, turning away from Duncan to face the boys. "Dust yourselves off, and let's head inside."

One pair of wide eyes stared at him with something other than obedience. He saw the sharp fear as clearly as if he'd heard the mental connection being made. The cop hadn't made it, but the kid sure had.

"A moment, if you please," Duncan growled behind him.

"Yes, sir?" Sam paused, hoping the acid churning in his stomach didn't show by so much as a flicker of an eyelash.

"You're new here, aren't you?"

Sam nodded. He kept from looking at the boy with an effort. Would the kid speak out? Did Duncan notice the sweat trickling down the side of Sam's face?

"You got a last name—Sam, was it?" The burly cop with the pockmarked face narrowed his eyes.

Just what Sam needed. A career cop with an attitude and a scared kid who could identify him.

"Moore."

"Moore, huh? Where you from, Mr. Moore?"

"Most recently? Utah."

"Utah." Officer Duncan savored the word. "Big place, Utah." He rocked back on his heels, raking Sam with a hard look. "Most recently, huh?"

Sam kept his expression blank, his fingers splayed at his sides, instead of curled with tension, the way they wanted to be. Any minute now, the boy would bolt, or condemn him with a word.

"Where, exactly, in Utah?"

Before Sam could answer, Carter's hearty greeting split the tension with effervescent friendliness. "Hey, there, Johnny D. How's it going?"

He strode across the yard from the main barn. Sam glimpsed Jake, watching from the recessed shadows inside the open doorway.

Duncan acknowledged the foreman, a bit reluctantly. "Carter."

"You'll have to excuse me," Sam told the men. To Carter he added, "I need to get the boys inside and organized for dinner."

"Sure. Go ahead. What brings you out our way, Johnny? Not more trouble, I hope."

Sam wanted to hear the answer to that, as well, but a grungy hand snagged his. Jerome looked up at him, his dark eyes filled with worry.

"Can we go inside now, Sam?"

"Sure thing. Okay, guys, let's move 'em out and move 'em in."

"Huh?" Mickey asked.

"He means get inside, dumbface," the boy called Hector answered.

"I knew that."

"Bull."

"Last one in gets the first bath," Sam told them. There was an instant rush toward the front porch. All except Jerome, who clung to Sam's hand and kept pace at his side.

MARLY LISTENED, her fingers pressed tightly against the hard plastic receiver.

"This is your last warning. Get rid of those kids before there's trouble." Almost immediately, the dial tone hummed in her ear. It took her several seconds to make herself replace the receiver.

Her heart stuttered in fear. This was by no means the first nasty call, but that didn't make it any less threatening. She turned blind eyes toward the window.

Damn it, she wasn't going to be a victim. If her so-called neighbors didn't like her horse farm, they should have bought houses elsewhere. Her place had been here long before the suburban sprawl moved in its direction, and working with troubled youths was something she had always wanted to do. She'd already taken steps to prevent the sort of problems that had occurred last year.

"Excuse me."

Her head snapped around. Sam leaned against the door frame to the office, the dirty duffel bag in one large hand. There was a sense of leashed power behind that negligent pose.

"Sorry to bother you, but the boys are upstairs getting ready for dinner. I'd like to know where I'm supposed to bunk for the night." Once again, the drawl was less pronounced.

This man was not what he seemed.

Marly straightened in her chair at the thought. "Come in. I take it you met Emma."

"Not to the point of introduction," Sam said wryly.

Marly had to smile. If she knew Emma, her stout friend had watched in silence when he brought the boys inside, and probably pointed down the hall when he asked for Marly. Emma used words with the care usually reserved for treasured artifacts.

"Emma's a dear. She doesn't talk much, but she cooks like a dream and manages to keep the house from being condemned by the health department."

"A noble effort, I'm sure."

Marly grinned in spite of herself, and motioned to one of the two red leather chairs opposite the desk. "Have a seat. I need to ask you a few questions."

Sam glanced around him. This was a man's room, dominated by dark paneling and heavy furniture. Marly was far too delicate for the padded leather chair behind the scarred oak desk. He wondered whose comfort the room had been intended for originally. Her ex-husband?

He dropped his bag next to the chair and sat down, trying not to let his stiffness show. Sam knew all about interrogation, from both sides of the table. His story would hold together. She didn't know who he was or why he was here, and he'd had years of experience telling lies in the name of undercover work. He waited for her to begin, without saying a word. Instead, he used the time to study the deceptively fragile lady sitting across from him. She had the most tempting lips set in that heart-shaped face.

"Are you wanted by the police?"

The question jerked him erect in the red leather chair. "Why would you ask a damn fool question like that?" Did she know? His words had sounded harsh, but at least he hadn't stammered in surprise.

"Look, Sam, I don't have time for more problems. I saw the way you reacted to Duncan. I want a straight answer."

His mind scrambled with alternatives as he forced himself to settle again. He tipped back his hat and stretched out his legs to cross them at the ankles. God only knew if he'd be able to uncross them afterward, but he had to look at ease.

Her eyes followed his movements. When she lifted them again and caught him watching, the faintest hint of a blush added color to her pale cheeks.

"In today's society, when a man chooses to be a drifter, he learns to be real wary of law officers. Sort of like your kids."

"What are you talking about?"

"Anything that goes wrong, it's the new guy people point fingers at. Cops don't like people like me. There's good reasons for that, I'll grant you, but it's the lifestyle I've chosen."

"Why?"

Sam shrugged. The easy lies tasted bitter in his mouth. For some reason, it was hard to lie to Marly. "Owning a spread takes money. I don't have any, but I like what I do."

"You could save to buy a place."

He thought about all his hard-earned money, sitting in several judicious investments, as well as his bank account. For just an instant, he wondered what it would have been like if he had done that very thing. He shrugged the thought aside.

"On what you pay? I don't think so." His grin came easily.

She studied him intently, as if she saw beneath his teasing words.

"I like my life," he continued. "It suits me. I get to see as much of the country as I want, with no one to nag at me except an occasional boss."

"How do you feel about kids?"

"As a species?"

"I'm serious, Sam."

"I can see that."

He could see other things, too—and he liked what he saw. She probably wouldn't care for his thoughts, but she was a pretty woman. There was too much character in her face for classic beauty, but she had flawless skin, especially for a woman who must work outside much of the time.

Marly leaned forward. "I'll come to the point. Our counselor quit last week. I haven't been able to find anyone else willing to spend the summer on a working horse farm. Carter can't do it all. I watched you with the boys today. They seem to respect you."

"I'm bigger than they are. They'd be foolish not to."

The fingers of her right hand drummed the desk. "You didn't answer my question. Do you like children?"

Sam debated his answer, not sure he wanted to follow the direction this was heading. He needed to talk to the kid at the first opportunity, find out what he'd seen that night, and then disappear before someone recognized him. "I never gave it much thought one way or another. Kids are just people on a smaller scale."

A flicker of a smile came and went. "You handle

them well, although I didn't like the way you pulled that knife earlier."

"There's a better way?"

She glared at him. "You know what I mean."

"No, ma'am, I'm not sure I do." He liked that she didn't back down from him. Her hazel eyes sparkled with challenge.

"These are inner-city kids. They see enough of that sort of thing on the streets. It's one of the reasons they're here—to be taught there's another way to live."

"My actions got their attention."

"Yes, I know—"

"Seemed to me the situation was gettin' out of hand." A lot like this conversation, he thought.

"The point is, I need someone to supervise the boys until I can find a replacement for the counselor."

"Me?"

"It pays more."

Right to the chase. Sam tilted his head, stalling for time as he weighed his options. "How much more?"

She named a figure. "Plus, you'll have your own bedroom, here inside the main house. You'll take your meals with the boys, and I already have lesson plans to work from."

Though she hid it well, her desperation pricked his conscience. Marly Kramer was a good woman. It didn't take a genius to see she was facing a lot of problems. He didn't want to add to them, but he knew he would. He wouldn't be here any longer than it took to get the information he needed.

"What sort of lesson plans?"

Marly reached for a pile of papers in the bin on the corner of the desk. "The counselor who left worked out a daily lesson plan for their entire stay."

"Whoa, wait a minute. You expect me to teach?" He wouldn't even be here a couple of days from now.

"No. Not at all. Well, not exactly."

"What, exactly?" His friends had always told him he had "sucker" emblazoned on his forehead.

"Just ranch stuff. How to ride, saddle a horse, that sort of thing."

He'd be a fool to turn her down. She was handing him a golden opportunity to get to the boy. The kid hadn't spoken up outside, but it was just a matter of time, now that he knew who Sam was. "Let me see these lesson plans."

She handed over a thick sheaf of papers. Sam brushed her hand as he took them, surprised again by his reaction to the touch of her skin. She pulled away quickly and swiped at her bangs. There were smudges of soot across her forehead and down one cheek that made him want to smile. Instead, Sam pulled his attention back to the papers in his hand.

"You gotta be kidding," he said after a moment. "I'm surprised this guy didn't write down times for potty breaks. Or aren't the boys supposed to have any?" Sam flicked through the pages without waiting for a response. "The person who wrote this crap obviously had a lot of time on his hands. Bet the boys loved him."

Marly shifted uncomfortably. "Well—"

"Never mind. I can imagine."

"You don't have to follow everything. I just thought this would give you a guide."

Sam cocked his head. "I don't think NASA has guidelines this tight."

Her chin lifted, and her lips tightened.

"Will you take the job, Sam? At least temporarily?

These kids need to see that something exists besides life in D.C."

He could have argued with her about what the kids *needed,* but what was the point? "Court-assigned?"

She lowered her eyes to study the desk blotter. She was afraid he wouldn't take the job, he realized.

"Yes. They've all been in trouble, but nothing serious. There's a panel that picks them—Judge Kirkland, Officer Porterfield, and two social workers. They decide which kids could benefit from a program like ours."

Porterfield.

The name sent a siren screaming through his head. Pieces of the puzzle slid neatly into place. Why hadn't he made the connection? He'd known about Bill's involvement in a program for troubled youths. Yet even when Sam learned the kid had been sent away, he hadn't put it together. If Bill was the dirty cop...

Sam wanted to explode with rage. It was Bill who had told them about the theft of the evidence. Bill, who'd sat in the bar that night and heard Sam state his destination. What could have been simpler than to follow Sam to the gym, break into his locker and exchange guns?

A simple frame. Use Sam's gun to murder the man whose testimony would convict Bill, plant some physical evidence in Sam's apartment, and *voilà,* off the hook and no one the wiser. Sam had made it all the neater by happening by at exactly the right moment and obligingly getting shot in the process.

Amazing, the risks Porterfield had taken. A lot of cops used that gym. He might have been seen at Sam's locker. Or, if Sam hadn't been so preoccupied, he might have noticed the gun switch right away, when he put on his holster that night.

Good old Bill of the endless diets. Hard to picture him as a dirty cop, let alone a murderer.

Sam's fingers balled into fists. Bill couldn't have guessed his patsy would skip, or that Sam would come up with the identity of the kid. And he wouldn't have, without help. The captain, who always played by the rules, friendship notwithstanding, had reluctantly given him that piece of information, mistakenly thinking it wouldn't matter.

"I've got a lead on the boy," George had told him gruffly.

Joe had stared at his friend in disbelief.

"Two brothers were picked up not far from the scene that night. The younger boy is the right age, and maybe, just maybe, he's your witness."

"Give me a name, George."

"Don't worry, I'll check him out."

"I want his name."

George had frowned and shook his head. "I know you're frustrated, but let me be sure he's the right one first. Then we'll turn this over to the investigators."

"What do you think I'm going to do, go chasing him down myself? These headaches are so bad I can still barely see straight."

George had clapped a hand on his shoulder in sympathy, his face speaking of the sleepless nights he was putting in on his friend's behalf. "I know. I'm sorry. I wish I could do more to help."

"The name?"

George had given him the name.

Bill probably thought he was safe. Certainly he thought the kid was out of reach. No one else, except George Brent and Sam, knew *who* the kid was. Only Bill had known *where* he was.

Until Sam had gotten lucky.

Now, Sam could barely contain the energy that surged through him. Bill should have remembered Sam's reputation for tenacity. He'd picked the wrong man to frame.

It was tough to stay slouched in the chair and focused on the current conversation. He forced his fingers to unclench. "You said you want references?" he asked Marly.

"Naturally." Soft, liquid eyes fringed by thick lashes regarded him steadily. Lines of strain were etched below and at the corners of her eyes. Lines that reminded Sam he wasn't the only one with problems. He just had to remember that his were the ones that counted.

A small body erupted through the open doorway without warning.

"Emma says you'd better come. Zeke's beatin' the crap outta Chris."

Chapter Three

Sam was on his feet before his muscles could protest. He followed Jerome down the hall and up the stairs, aware of Marly on his heels. The other boys were clustered outside the bedroom, watching the combatants.

Blood dripped from one nose, while the other boy sported the start of a black eye. Sam grabbed the back of the nearest shirt and pulled, while Marly pinned the other boy's arms to his sides.

"The fight's over," Marly told them decisively. Fortunately, both were more than ready to quit. She looked at the four faces in the doorway. "Finish washing up and go downstairs."

Sam released his captive and motioned to the nearest bed. "Sit," he commanded. "You're Zeke?"

"Yeah." The sable-haired youngster wiped futilely at his bloody nose. "But he started it."

"Did not. You said—"

"I don't care." Sam didn't raise his voice. He didn't have to. He knew exactly which tone to adopt to silence them. "You two want to expend all that energy beatin' each other to a pulp, that's your business."

He heard the sound of Marly's indrawn breath as she

stepped out of the bathroom with a wet washcloth. He took it from her without looking up. "Thanks."

Sam spotted Emma hovering in the doorway uncertainly.

"Emma, we could use some ice for Chris's eye."

Emma disappeared.

"Okay, guys, let me tell you how this is gonna work from now on." As he talked, he took one of Zeke's grungy fingers and pressed it and the cloth up against the narrow band of skin and cartilage between the nostrils. "Push against that spot. Yeah. Like that. Tilt your head a little, now. Good. Now then, you guys want to fight, that's fine with me, but we'll do it by the rules."

"Rules? What rules? There's no rules in fighting."

"There is around here. You want to learn how to fight, I'll teach you."

"Sam!"

He didn't look at Marly.

"But you have to do it my way."

"What's your way? Sissy gloves and a ring?" Zeke demanded with a sneer.

"Nope. I've never boxed, so I don't know much about it. Besides, boxing's a sport. Fighting isn't."

"So what's your way?"

Emma bustled in, holding two towel-wrapped bundles of ice.

"Thanks, Emma. Put this on your eye," he told Chris.

"Ow! It's cold!"

"Takes the swelling down. It's easier to fight if you can see out of both eyes."

"Sam..." Marly protested again.

This time he did look at her, and he had the strangest urge to kiss those prim lips. He turned back to his young charge, pulled away the washcloth and positioned the other makeshift ice pack.

"Did you say dinner was almost ready, Emma? The boys and I need to have a little chat first, but I don't want to miss whatever it is you're cooking down there. The smells are close to heaven."

Emma was startled into a grin. Her plump face was surprisingly pretty when she smiled. "Three minutes," she told him.

"Good. Marly, would you take the other boys…?"

"I'm not going anywhere."

"Okay. You want to learn how to fight, too?"

Zeke snickered.

"Oh, I know how to fight," she told him, hands on her trim hips. "I just don't use my fists."

His lips twitched in amusement. "I like the sounds of that."

She looked pointedly at the kids. "Only because you don't know any better."

He tipped his head in acknowledgment and turned back to the boys. "You two need to get washed up for supper."

"But don't you care who started it?" Zeke demanded.

"Nope. I ended it. Remember that. Rule number one—it doesn't matter who starts a fight, only who walks away the winner. In this case, it's me. You both lost. Got it?"

He stared them down. Two heads bobbed unwillingly. "Then let's get in the bathroom and get this bleeding stopped."

"I need to talk to you," Marly told him.

"Can it wait until after dinner, boss? We've only got two minutes, according to Emma, and it'll take both of them to get these two presentable. I'll meet you down-stairs. Bathroom in here?"

He was amazed she let him get away with it. He could feel her gaze on him as he strode toward the bath-room after the two kids. Fortunately, the nosebleed was almost stopped. Chris tried to leave after he washed his hands and face, but Sam set him smartly down on the toilet seat. The boy watched him warily from his one good eye, the makeshift ice pack covering the other one.

"All right, Zeke. Go change your shirt and then head downstairs. I want to talk to Chris for a minute."

Zeke smirked.

"But he started it," Chris protested.

"I told you I don't care about that. I want to talk to you about something else. Get a move on, Zeke."

Dismay plastered Chris's face as Zeke left for his own room. "We need to talk," Sam told Chris.

"About what?" Apprehension pitched his voice up an octave.

"You were there, that night." Alarm spread across the small face. He knew exactly what night Sam was referring to. "I almost shot you."

Chris turned away, breathing hard. "I don't know what you're talkin' about."

Sam hunkered down to be on a more equal footing with him, but Chris wouldn't look at him. "I need your help, Chris. I'm in big trouble."

The small mouth pinched in silence. The kid was scared to death.

"Look, you don't have to come forward and testify or anything. All I need is a name. A description. I never got a good look at the guy, but you were there. You saw who pulled the trigger."

Chris gave a ragged shake of his head. "I don't know what you're talkin' about, man."

"Chris, they're going to set me down for murder if you don't help me."

"I didn't see nothin'!" Chris blurted out. He scooted off the seat and backed away when Sam would have touched him. The boy wasn't just scared, he was terrified.

"Chris, I'm not going to hurt you."

His eyes all but rolled in fear. "We're late for dinner. Marly won't like it." The words came out high and shrill. The small body quaked. Sam flexed his fingers and stood. He'd known this wasn't going to be easy.

"All right. We'll talk about it later. Let's go."

Chris scampered past him and tore out of the room. Sam followed more slowly, swallowing his tension. Time was his enemy, yet that was what he needed to win the boy's trust.

Downstairs, Emma stood in the doorway, holding a large platter. Everyone else was already seated, and they looked up expectantly. Particularly Marly. His mother used to wear that look, Sam remembered. It had never boded well.

"Sorry to be late," he said.

Emma beamed and moved forward. Marly continued to stare. Reluctantly Sam removed his hat. Marly's eyes fastened at once on the angry red scar that angled along his forehead, over the left temple. There was no way for her to know it had been made by a bullet. Only she was a bright lady. How long would it take her to put the pieces together and come up with the fact that she was harboring a fugitive?

As Sam sat down across from Marly and began filling his plate, he caught another pair of eyes that traced the bullet's path. Chris looked down quickly at the dinner plate in front of him. Sam could almost feel the kid's raw fear.

He knew Marly hadn't missed the boy's reaction, either. It was obvious that she was as puzzled by it as she was curious about the scar. Fortunately, she didn't ask questions, and the kids began to eat as though faced with imminent starvation. There was silence for several minutes, broken only by the clink of silverware and the sounds of contented eating. Sam caught Marly watching him, a speculative look on her face. It was almost a relief when one of the boys began to talk.

"Sam's gonna teach us how to fight," Zeke announced around a mouthful of chicken. The words produced an immediate chorus of approval from the other boys.

Sam gave a mental groan and looked down the table, into turbulent hazel eyes. An "I told you so" expression was already in place. The words just hadn't made it to her lips yet.

"Yeah. Next time Chris calls me a fathead, I'm gonna—"

"Whoa, now. Didn't I tell you there were rules?" Sam waved his fork, amazed by Marly's restraint. He had the distinct impression that she wanted to be chewing on him instead of her food. "There are better ways to settle problems."

Disgusted frowns appeared as the boys waited for Parental Lecture 101. Aware that Marly was close to interrupting, Sam stabbed a bite of chicken. "I'll tell you about a few of the more interesting ones later on. For now, what did I tell you is rule number one?"

"The one who walks away is the winner," Zeke stated with pride.

"Right. Now, who here thinks they can take me on and win?"

"You mean in a fight? With fists?" one of the boys demanded.

"That's right."

"You're too big," Jerome protested.

"Exactly." Sam set down his fork and studied the faces looking up at his.

"That brings me to rule number two. I'm bigger than you guys, so I'm gonna win all the fights around here."

"We aren't gonna fight with you," Mickey protested.

"Which brings me to rule number three. Any fight you guys have from now on involves me. Remember rule number two? That means you guys always lose the fight."

"That's stupid."

There was grumbling agreement.

"Sam," Marly said, so sweetly he wanted to wince. "We need to have a talk."

"Absolutely," he agreed cheerfully, wondering how he was going to get out of this one. Marly frowned, and he quickly asked one of the boys to pass him the vegetable platter, hoping to divert her.

From somewhere came the sound of a telephone. Marly jumped, looking snakebit. Emma frowned and rose to her feet. She reappeared in the doorway a minute or so later without saying a word.

"Excuse me," Marly said, setting down her napkin. She rose from the table, as if reluctant. Sam had to force himself to nod and not ask questions. It was none of his business what her problems were. He had his own troubles to deal with. His appetite was dust all of a sudden.

"Anybody want more chicken?" he asked. No one

did. The boys had made large inroads into the meal. Even Chris had eaten well. Marly hadn't returned by the time the kids started getting antsy. He was wondering what to do with them when Emma rose and disappeared into the kitchen. She returned a second later, standing in the doorway, a cake plate in her hands.

"Emma? Any chance you could serve that chocolate cake outside on the front porch, so I can demonstrate a few defensive moves to the boys?" Sam asked.

Emma nodded.

"Let's go!" Donald said amid the scramble as the boys started to jump up.

Sam gave a loud whistle. The small bodies stopped moving instantly. "Sit." At his sharp command, they collapsed onto their chairs. "Is that how you leave a dinner table?" Six pairs of eyes stared at him without comprehension.

"Thank you for dinner, Emma. Your chicken is the best I've tasted in a long while."

The boys looked at him in confusion.

Jerome frowned, staring at Sam. Sam tilted his head in Emma's direction. "Oh. Uh, thanks for dinner, Emma."

There was a low chorus of mumbled thanks. Emma fairly beamed. "You may carry your dishes to the kitchen, and then you're excused," Sam told them. The room erupted again as eager bodies lunged to obey.

Marly stood in the doorway, a pleased but thoughtful look on her face. Her tension had evaporated, so the phone call must not have been what she feared.

"Do you want to explain what you're doing?" Marly asked.

"Teachin' them some manners."

"I mean outside."

"I'm going to show the boys a few self-defense moves."

"Self-defense."

"Yeah, you know." He took a long step in her direction. "Someone enters your space—" he stood close enough to notice the way her pulse sped up in her throat "—and you don't want to give ground—" the way she was refusing to do at the moment "—but you want the other person to move away."

Her eyes flicked to his face, trying to measure his intent, but she didn't step back. "I don't think fighting is listed anywhere on those lesson plans I gave you earlier," she said firmly.

"Probably not. Anyone who had time to write up all that junk probably wouldn't know how to remove someone from his space."

She reached up with the flats of both hands to push him away. Sam didn't move. Her eyes opened expressively.

"Looks like you could use a few of my lessons, too," he murmured. She'd forgotten to drop her hands. Sam liked the feel of them against his chest.

She tipped her head to one side. "Or I could show you what I can do with my knee."

Sam grinned. "Let's save that demonstration for later, shall we?" He could smell the clean scent of her shampoo, and he had a ridiculous urge to reach out and pull on her silky ponytail. "Make up your mind, Marly. Do you want me to work with the boys or not?"

"I don't want you to teach them how to fight. They already know how to do that."

"They know how to hurt each other, and that's a dead end. Give me a chance, Marly."

From the corner of his eye, he caught sight of Emma.

Her chins bounced up and down in agreement. Sam realized he had one person in his corner.

Marly hadn't missed the action, either. With a sigh, she dropped her hands and stepped back. "I must be out of my mind."

He reached out and touched the tip of her nose. The insignificant act sent a wave of current up his arm. It was all he could do not to bend down and taste those provocative lips.

"Don't worry about it. Obviously, my mind must be out there wandering around someplace, too. Come on. I need a victim."

It was a mistake, Sam discovered. He should never have used Marly for his demonstration partner. He was going to sleep with the scent and feel of her skin uppermost in his mind tonight. Positioning her for the various throws shot his concentration all to hell. All he could feel was the supple firmness of her body and the softness of her skin. All he could smell was the light fragrance of her shampoo. Sam was worried the boys were going to get another sort of lesson altogether before he was through.

Three and a half hours later, they had the last body inside the proper room and prepared for bed. Sam had pulled all-night stakeouts that weren't this exhausting. He tried hard not to think about what the boys were really doing behind those closed doors. He rubbed the back of his neck and wished for a hot bath, a cold beer and a bottle of antacid.

Despite his best efforts to find another chance to talk to Chris, the kid had displayed enough savvy not to give him any openings. Marly had seemed to watch both of them closely.

"Everything all right?"

He turned, startled to find her eying him from the top step of the staircase.

"Sorry," she said quietly. "I didn't mean to scare you."

"No problem. I was just wondering where I was supposed to bunk down for the night. You did say inside the house, didn't you?"

She'd obviously forgotten that. He hadn't. He watched while she made up her mind.

MARLY STARED at his rugged features. His expression was completely unreadable. "Right here." She indicated the door beside him.

Until that moment, she hadn't decided whether to send him to the bunkhouse with the other men or let him stay inside with her.

"Next to the steps, huh? Is that so I can hear if the boys decide to sneak out?"

Marly bit down on her lips for a moment, surprised by his perceptiveness. "Are you a sound sleeper?"

"Nope."

"Good."

He frowned. "Are you worried one of them will actually try to sneak away?"

"No."

She knew she'd said it too fast. Her eyes slithered away from contact with his.

"Where's your room?"

Marly lifted her chin. Her heart tripped quickly. "Across from yours."

"Convenient."

"Not in this lifetime, cowboy."

Sam tipped his head, a trace of a smile curling the corners of his lips. "I meant, in case one of our desperadoes decides to escape. We'll have 'em in a cross fire.''

Marly didn't smile back, disturbed anew by the appeal this man held for her. "Let's go down to my office. There are a few things we need to discuss."

She felt him behind her as she made her way down the stairs, wondering all the while if she was making a mistake. Was she letting him stay inside because of the things his past employer had said, or because he was so good with the boys? Or was there another, more primitive reason?

Marly shook aside the last thought. There was a single light on in the den. She made a point of turning on two more before she settled behind the oversize desk.

"I called that number in Utah you gave me. Mrs. Norton was effusive in her praise of you and your work. She said to be sure and tell you that you could have a job with her husband and her anytime you need one."

Sam settled back, with an expression that said he hadn't expected anything less. "Good folks" was all he said.

Marly bit down on her lower lip and stared at the dark painting on the wall behind Sam's head. Actually, Mrs. Norton had talked about Sam as if he were a part of her family. It had been a very reassuring conversation. No doubt it was the main reason she had offered him the room inside the house.

"You okay?"

Sam's easy drawl brought her focus back to his face.

"I'm fine." She took a steadying breath and leaned back in the chair, trying to mimic his relaxed pose. "Here's the deal. Your job is to keep tabs on the boys. Keep them occupied. Use the lesson plans if you need guidance. From time to time I'll need you for other duties, but your primary responsibility will be the boys. Got it?''

''Sounds clear enough.''

''They aren't bad kids,'' she told him.

''No more than I'm a bad drifter,'' he agreed.

She forced her teeth to release her bottom lip. Bad? Ha! That was part of the problem. Sam Moore was dangerously attractive. He was also good with the boys. Part of her wanted to trust him, confide her problems and ask his advice. The sane part of her jeered at her foolishness and told her to get her mind back on business.

''Did you know your drawl fades in and out?''

She'd succeeded in unsettling him again, she saw. He sat up quickly, wincing slightly, and shook his head.

''You ask the damnedest questions.''

She kept her smile inside. ''That isn't an answer.''

''I believe I've mentioned that I travel extensively. I pick up speech patterns from everywhere.'' He settled himself in his chair again and stared at her. ''Let me ask you something. Why did Duncan show up here this afternoon?''

''Officer Duncan lives in the new housing development on the old Ripcott farm, down the street. Last year there were some problems with the neighborhood kids.''

''His kids?''

Marly shrugged. ''Among others. He's part of the campaign to close me down. Or at least my youth program.''

''Hmm… Why did Carter lie to you today?''

She shifted uncomfortably under his steady gaze. ''He has a misguided need to protect me. He and I have already had words about that.''

''Does Officer Duncan own a pickup truck?''

Marly glared at him. Just who was interrogating whom? "You sound like a cop," she said accusingly. Was it her imagination, or did he flinch?

"Come on, Marly. That isn't an answer." His mouth turned up at the corners, letting her know he was mimicking her earlier words to him.

She debated responding, but the possibilities behind his question invited speculation. "Are you saying you think Duncan pulled down my fence? A respected officer of the law?"

"Nope. Not in that capacity, certainly. But as an irate neighbor? Who knows?"

"That's crazy."

"Maybe."

Marly couldn't interpret Sam's expression, but he had planted more than a kernel of suspicion. Could Officer Duncan be behind her problems? It would explain a lot.

"What are you thinking?"

"Duncan doesn't like me," she answered automatically. "He and my husband didn't get along. Last summer his son was hauled in with a group of kids from here when they attempted to break into the local school."

Sam quirked an eyebrow. "*Into* a school?"

"I know. Crazy, huh? No damage was done and charges were dropped, but it probably didn't do much to enhance Duncan's standing with the other county cops."

"I wouldn't imagine so."

"His whole family is on the police force. His brother's a cop, his sister's a dispatcher, and his father is a retired sergeant."

"Have you thought about relocating?" he asked with a touch of irony.

"Yes."

She'd given it a lot of thought lately, but her abrupt answer seemed to surprise him. Sam uncrossed his legs and started to stand. He moved stiffly. Was it because of the accident that had injured his head, or because he wasn't used to riding and hard labor, as he claimed?

"Well, as much fun as this has been—"

Marly interrupted him. "How'd you get that scar?"

"Some people might call that question nosy." He towered over her desk.

Marly refused to be intimidated. "Some people might not be trying to protect themselves."

He cocked his head to one side. "From me?"

"If necessary. Is it necessary, Sam?"

His smile was lethal. No doubt she was going to dream about those dark brown eyes.

"Nope. But I assume your bedroom door has a lock?"

The question shocked her. That was probably exactly what he'd intended, she realized. "You're trying to distract me."

He regarded her with a naughty expression that sent inexplicable tingles of excitement singing through her body. She would not rise to his bait, but she couldn't control the fine tremors in her hands, so she clasped them together in front of her on the desk.

"Is it working?" he asked.

Better than he could possibly know. Heat flashed through her at his expression. Heat, and images best left unthought. "No. It isn't going to work."

"On the contrary, I think we'll work very well together, Marly."

She shook her head, as much to dispel the enchantment his tone tried to weave as in denial of the words themselves. "It's an empty threat, cowboy. I can see right through you."

"Really?"

"You're no more interested in me than I am in Carter. You're just trying to distract me from more questions."

"Interesting."

"What is?"

"That you mention Carter. He warned me off you earlier today."

"What?" Flabbergasted, she closed her mouth and shoved back her chair, anger pulsing through her. "What did he say?"

Sam tipped his head. "Just that you were off-limits. I asked him if that applied to him, as well, but apparently not."

An angry denial sprang to her lips. She caught the words just in time. He was playing with her, like a cat with its prey.

Marly stood and came around the desk with a rueful smile. "You're good, Sam. I'll concede this round. You don't want to tell me about your past, that's fine—as long as it doesn't interfere with your duties or my business." She would have sworn that was admiration in his eyes.

"Breakfast is at seven," she told him. "Be on time, please."

"I'm never late for meals."

She'd stepped too close to him, she realized. She could reach out and touch him. Her fingers remembered the feel of his broad chest. He smelled faintly of horses and sweat, and Sam. No artificial scents for this man. She was surprised to find she liked that.

"Good night, Sam."

There was definitely approval in his face. Approval

and something else. Something that triggered a feminine response she was hopeless to stop. With two fingers, he reached out and traced a path down the side of her face, leaving prickles of awareness in their wake.

"A man would be a fool," he said softly, "not to be interested in you."

Her breath caught in her throat. For just a moment, she thought he was going to kiss her. Then he turned and strode out of the room.

Marly stood still for several long heartbeats. She released the breath she'd been holding in a rush of air and stared unseeing at the picture on the far wall. Sam Moore was *definitely* not what he pretended to be.

THE TELEPHONE RANG for so long Sam was about to give up when a sleep-filled voice finally snarled a hello in his ear.

"Wake up, partner. I need some help," Sam said.

A string of oaths followed that announcement. Enough to tell him Lee was awake and cognizant of his caller.

"I don't believe it. I don't effing believe it. Where the hell are you? Are you okay? What are you doing calling me at—at three o'clock in the morning? Are you out of your—?"

"Are you awake yet?"

"Yes, I'm awake. Are you okay?"

"Fine. I was set up."

"Hell, I know that. How long have we worked together? I told them that, Joe, over and over and over again. The fools wouldn't listen."

"Do they know who was on the take yet?"

"Sure they do. They have you nicely fingered."

It was Sam's turn to curse. "Are they looking any further?"

"Of course they are. None of us take a leak that we aren't being watched. They've probably got this line tapped."

"Not likely." It was a local call, and Sam didn't figure it was too big a risk. "You know what the budget looks like. Most of us are going to be lucky to take home a paycheck until the D.C. government gets its act together."

"True. And I'm glad you said 'us.'" Lee's smooth voice traveled over the line reassuringly. "What do you need?"

"Information on Porterfield."

"Porterfield? Why? You think Bill—? Nah. No way. You're barking up the wrong tree. He's as clean as a virgin."

"How many virgins do you know, Lee?"

His partner snorted. Then his voice grew thoughtful. "Porterfield. Jesus. What do you want to know? IA probably even knows the details of his diets."

"He's working with a youth program."

"So?"

"Find out as much as you can about it."

"Why?"

"Lee." He expelled the name in exasperation.

"Okay, okay. Anything in particular?"

"Yeah. I want to know about this summer school program. Where do the kids come from? Who picks them? Does he have contact with them outside the program?"

"What has this got to do with Rayback?"

Sam scratched his bristly jaw, wishing he could

shave. "Nothing directly. I'm working an angle. I'm sure IA is covering everyone's finances."

"Tighter than an IRS audit."

Something in Lee's tone alerted him. "You okay, buddy?"

"Yeah. Sure. They're going to attach my wages. Seems my greedy little ex wants her back alimony in blood. I'm setting a bad example, you know."

Sam sighed, wishing he could help. Lee's recent divorce had been a real eye-opener to the few single men in their unit. Greedy was an understatement when used to describe his ex-wife. The best lawyer had won—big-time.

"Sorry, Lee."

"Yeah. Me too. There goes my vacation in Tahiti," he said sarcastically.

"It's probably a tourist trap, anyhow."

"Yeah. Give me a number where I can reach you."

"You can't. I'm on the move." He didn't dare put Lee or himself in any more jeopardy than necessary. "I'll call you back in a day or so."

"You sure you're okay? The head?"

"Solid as a rock."

"Damn good thing, or you'd be dead right now."

"Tell me about it."

"The captain's pretty worried about you, Joe."

"Are you asking why I called you instead of him?"

"Hell, no. He'd trace the call and turn you in for your own good." There was a strange bitterness underscoring those words. "We all know George is a by-the-book cop."

"He giving you guys a hard time?"

"Hey, who needs to sleep?"

As captain, George Brent had probably been jumping

down everyone's throats since Sam disappeared, and Lee was right—at this point, George would turn him in. Then he'd continue to bust his ass trying to prove Sam's innocence.

"Sorry, Lee."

"Hey, no problem. I'll do what I can."

"I know. Thanks."

Sam replaced the phone and leaned back against the chair in Marly's den. He stared around the dark room, wanting to turn on a light. You could learn a lot about a person by going through her desk. Still, he was taking enough of a chance as it was.

He was bone-tired and sore all over. Working out didn't use the same muscles as riding horses and hauling fence posts. He considered spending the rest of the night right here in this chair, instead of expending the effort it would take to get up. A tempting idea, but impossible. There'd be no way to explain his presence in the morning.

Sam struggled to his feet and navigated his way to the room at the top of the stairs. He paused for just a moment to study Marly's closed door.

What did she dream of? And what did she wear to bed? With a sigh, he opened his door and stepped inside.

His room reminded him of a hotel, with its clean, almost sterile appearance. The sturdy maple furniture was old and obviously used, but buffed to a bright shine. Sam didn't even mind that the connecting bathroom was shared by two miniature adults. The room contained the one essential ingredient, as far as he was concerned. A full-size bed.

Sam stripped off his jeans and tumbled back onto the

freshly scented sheets, pulling the covers over him with a flick of his hand. In moments, he was asleep.

He came fully awake sometime later, alert to every sound, straining to hear whatever it was that had disturbed his sleep. He lay on his side, with his back to the door. It was an effort to keep his breathing slow and even.

He was no longer alone in the room.

With his heart thundering against his chest, his fingers crept toward the pillow beneath his head. A tiny whisper of cloth. Something lightly tapped his bared shoulder. He whipped upward in a flurry of motion, his gun in one hand, even as he swung around toward the intruder.

"Sam?"

He released the bony arm and fistful of cloth he had grabbed and lowered the weapon. His breath came out in a ragged sound as adrenaline sought an outlet. Small, terrified eyes regarded him. Only the whites reflected in the dark room.

"I'm sorry. I didn't mean it," the child whimpered. The boy had taken a defensive crouch, hands raised to ward off the expected blows.

For just a second, Sam thought he would vomit. He flicked the safety on again, and slid the gun out of sight. His hands were shaking badly, he noticed. And so they should be.

"Jerome. It's okay. I'm sorry." He forced himself to speak slowly, quietly, while his heart continued to race. "You scared me," he explained. A horrendous understatement.

The arms dropped timidly from around his face, but Jerome continued to crouch against the nightstand. "I didn't mean to. Honest."

"I know, son. It's okay. Come here."

With painful slowness, the boy stood erect. There was a tear in the T-shirt he wore. Sam swallowed back bile, along with his self-directed curses and wished he could manage a smile for the boy. It was beyond him at this moment.

"I'm sorry, Jerome. What's wrong?"

Jerome wouldn't meet his gaze. Sam reached over to turn on the light, flinching when the boy cringed backward again.

"Are you okay, son?"

The small head bobbed once. Sam reached out and rubbed his kinky hair. It was quarter to five, according to the clock on the nightstand.

"Did you have a bad dream?" If not, Sam had undoubtedly given him a new one.

"No."

Sam waited. The wariness faded from Jerome's expression, but not the worry that pinched that small face.

"He's gone," Jerome said finally.

Acid mingled with the cold fear in the pit of his stomach. "Who's gone?"

But Sam knew. His gut knew. It couldn't be anyone else, and he had no one to blame but himself.

"Chris. He's gone. I think someone took him."

Chapter Four

"Why do you think someone took Chris?" The cold fear hardened to solid ice. It was all Sam could do to keep his voice low and steady.

"Because it's dark out," Jerome told him reasonably. "He wouldn't go out while it's dark out."

Sam expelled a long breath of air. It was okay. Maybe. Please, Lord, it had to be okay. "Jerome, how long has Chris been gone?"

His shoulders heaved in a deep shrug. "I just woke up an' he was gone."

Sam tugged on his jeans. "Maybe he went to the bathroom."

"Nope. I already looked. He ain't down in the kitchen, neither."

"Jerome, think about this. Carefully." He pulled on a shirt, fumbling with the buttons. "Did Chris say anything to you? Anything at all that might give me a clue as to where he'd go?"

"Nope."

Fear gnawed on his insides. He had to believe the boy was simply hiding, but the alternative lurked in his mind, casting horrible images. "Was he upset tonight? Nervous? Scared?"

Dark eyes stared back at him. Once again the bony shoulders shrugged. "I don't know."

"Okay. It's okay, kid. We'll find him." Sam stood and reached for his gun, positioning his body so that Jerome wouldn't notice what he was doing. "He can't have gone far."

Jerome's head waggled agreement. "It's dark out."

"Yeah. But not for long." Sam snatched up his denim jacket.

Chris wasn't afraid of the dark. Sam knew that for a fact. If Chris ran away, where would he go? The nearest housing development was two miles down the road. Town was over eight miles away. This was a city kid. Country roads were a lot darker than city streets.

Unless he wasn't alone.

Sam couldn't stop thinking about that.

Maybe the barn? It would be an obvious place for a boy to hide until daylight.

He ignored the inner voice that berated him for not pulling Chris aside again tonight. He should have reassured the boy. Or maybe he should have scared the kid into talking to him. But that wasn't his style. Chris was already scared. Sam had thought there was time to earn the boy's trust, to get him to talk freely. Later, he could curse himself for not anticipating this. Right now, he had a child to find. One who might be lost, but was definitely scared.

And that was most certainly Sam's fault.

Sam grabbed his hat. "Come on, kid. We're going back to your room. It's too early to get up."

"What about Chris?"

"I'll find him." *I have to find him,* he admitted to himself.

In the boys' bedroom, there was no sign that Chris

had been taken against his will. As Jerome climbed into bed, Sam checked through the clothing and personal items hanging in the closet. Since he didn't know what belonged to Chris and he didn't want to chance upsetting the now calm, sleepy-eyed boy, he couldn't tell if anything was missing. Knowing he needed to stay calm, Sam restrained his growing fear.

He made a careful, quiet search of the upstairs. All the other boys were accounted for. Downstairs, the first thing he discovered was that the front door was unlocked. Doubts assailed him. There was no sign the lock had been forced. It was a good, solid deadbolt. Maybe Marly hadn't locked it. For all he knew, Marly never locked her doors. Or maybe Chris had unlocked it when he left. Certainly Porterfield wouldn't have a key.

Would he?

Sam stepped outside. A three-quarter moon hung low in the sky, shedding enough illumination to see by. Thick beads of dew clung heavily to the blades of grass in the damp, chill air. There was no sign that footprints had disturbed the lawn. Of course, a person could have stayed on the hard-packed earth, or he could have passed over the grass before the dew formed.

How long had Chris been gone?

Sam studied the scene carefully before he began to circle the house, staying on the wide front porch and skirting the rockers, chairs and small tables that invited a person to sit. If only Chris had.

The porch wrapped the left side of the house, culminating at a wide-open deck in the backyard, with two brick barbecue grills built onto one end. Sam's footsteps showed damply against the wood grain of the decking. No one else had walked across it recently.

The long, low bunkhouse, formerly a stable, stretched

behind the house, dark and silent as the night. He sighed and jumped off the deck, heading for the barn. He was glad for his jacket. The air had a decided chill to it.

Was Chris warm enough?

A low nicker greeted him when he pushed his way inside the main barn. The earthy smells of horses and hay brought a surge of memories, but Sam pushed them aside as he moved from stall to stall, stroking a muzzle here, patting a long neck arched in curiosity there.

In a barn this size, there were any number of places a small boy could hide. His search was no longer a one-man job. He needed to rouse help. Marly couldn't be any more upset with him than he already was with himself.

A sound, quickly muffled from overhead, stopped him in his tracks as he was about to turn and leave. Sam eyed the nearest ladder climbing to the loft. Of course. The perfect place. Huge hay bales were stacked to the rafters. There were makeshift aisles between the stacks. Plenty of cubbyholes up there for a boy to hide in. Sam had done it himself when he was a kid.

He climbed quickly. "Chris?"

It was a risk. Chris was more apt to flee than to come at the sound of his voice.

"It's okay, son. Come on out."

He heard a rustle of movement off to his left. Sam turned in that direction and brushed against a tower of hay. A sneeze began to build in his chest. Hay dust. He'd forgotten his allergy to the substance. It had grown worse over the years. Now he suppressed a sneeze and strode along the wall of hay.

"No one's going to hurt you, Chris. I promise. We need to talk about—"

Sam bowed his head under the force of the sneeze.

The gesture saved his life. With a whistle of displaced air, the huge metal hook used to raise and lower the bales swung over the top of the pile, into the path where he would have been walking if he hadn't stopped. It was so close, the metal hook pulled the hat from his head.

Instantly Sam went into a defensive crouch as the hook swung like a pendulum, back the way it had come. There was a series of rapid noises. Footsteps, other sounds. Noises not made by an eleven-year-old kid, but maybe made by someone intent on harming that same kid?

He reached for the gun tucked in the back of his jeans. Without warning, the pile of hay alongside him tumbled down. There was no chance to get out of its path. With his hand caught reaching behind him, Sam was off balance. He sprawled against the wood planks, pinned under the weight of several bales.

He was saved from serious injury by the narrowness of the aisle. Sneezing violently, he struggled to free himself, even as he listened to the sound of his attacker escaping down the other ladder. There was a whinny of protest from below as horses objected to being disturbed.

Sam rubbed at his eyes. They were itchy and burning. Another sneeze just about doubled him over. He needed to get out of here. His hand landed on his crushed Stetson. He worked to free it from the hay that pinned it to the floor. It took several more minutes to locate his gun, which had fallen from his fingers.

A small scuffling sound caught his attention.

"Chris?"

There was no response to his shout, but the noise

came again. He had to check the other side of this wall of hay. Chris might be there. Something was still there.

Was Chris tied up?

Or injured?

Sam pulled at the bales of hay before he realized he'd have to backtrack to find another path. His eyes watered, but the skittering noise drew him on. There was a soft bleat.

Sam rounded a corner, ready for anything. Anything except the sight of a tiny baby goat, penned in by a circle of hay bales. The animal made a pitiful sound of distress. Someone had wrapped the beast in a harness. There was a metal ring on the top of the wrapping. It took Sam a moment to understand what he was seeing.

That same someone had planned to suspend the young goat in the center of the barn using the hook. His stomach clenched. The implied threat was obvious.

"Chris!" He couldn't keep the demand from his voice. Was the boy up here? Had he seen the person with the goat? If so, he could be in danger from this new source as well.

"Chris, answer me. Make a noise if you're up here."

Nothing. He sneezed again, unable to hear another thing beyond the restless sounds of the horses below and the goat in front of him. A sheet of paper caught his eyes. It was clear across the makeshift goat pen, but even from his angle he could see the cutout letters pasted to the paper.

Sam uttered an expletive and sneezed violently. His skin was beginning to itch. He had to get out of here, but first he needed to see what the paper said. Was the warning intended for him, for Chris, or for Marly?

The goat bleated. At a guess, the animal was only a few weeks old. Sam swung over the barrier and into the small clearing. The goat butted forlornly against his leg as he bent to read the paper.

Next time it will be another kind of kid.

Sam uttered a curse and wiped at his eyes. The threat being aimed at Marly didn't make him feel the least bit better. Where was Chris? Had he seen the perpetrator getting ready to hang the goat? Was he hiding from Sam, or was he in trouble?

A sneeze hurt his chest, which was tightening alarmingly. He really had to get out of here. He patted the tiny animal even as he stepped over the bale of hay.

"Sorry, guy. I'll send someone to set you free in a minute."

Outside, he paused in an effort to fill his lungs with the clean night air, while trying to stop the sneezes that gripped him. Through itchy, runny eyes, he peered around at the silent yard. The perp was long gone, but Sam was in no position to give chase—at the moment, anyhow. His allergy was worse than he remembered, but fear overrode that consideration.

He had to find Chris. There was danger out here. Maybe a murderer, as well.

"MARLY. Wake up."

She rolled instinctively to face those husky words, a smile of welcome on her lips.

"Marly!"

Marly blinked her eyes open as the light alongside her bed winked on. A violent sneeze wiped away the last vestiges of sleep. Sam towered over her, but this was not the Sam of her erotic dreams. This Sam was abrupt and angry and covered in bits of hay. Even as she tried to assimilate this, he began to sneeze again.

"Good Lord, what happened to you?" She slid off the far side of the bed, pulling on her robe, without waiting for a response. His face was blotchy. His eyes were puffy and red. Tears streamed down his cheeks, unchecked.

"Get those clothes off," she ordered.

"Thanks, boss, another time," he managed to get out between sneezes. She could hear a slight wheezing in his chest that scared the heck out of her.

"Chris is missing," he continued.

"What?" Her heart fluttered in fear. Sam sneezed again.

One emergency at a time. Being allergic to bee stings herself, Marly knew the importance of prompt treatment for allergic reactions. She kept an injection kit for just such emergencies.

"I'll get the epinephrine."

He stopped her with a hand. "Antihistamine. I can breathe."

"Yeah, but for how long?"

"Antihistamine."

She came around the bed. "Are you sure?"

"We have to find Chris."

Marly nodded. She opened the drawer in her bedroom dresser and pushed aside underwear, searching for the packet of antihistamines she had stuffed in there one day when she was in a hurry. Her hands moved rapidly as her mind raced. Chris was missing.

"You ought to change clothes. What were you doing, rolling in the hay?"

"Literally," Sam muttered.

He took the two tablets she held out and swallowed

them dry. Only then did she realize what she'd said. Sam sneezed again before she could be embarrassed.

"Go and change. You won't do Chris any good if you go into anaphylactic shock. Do you know where he went? Have you checked the house?"

"Not thoroughly," he said with a shake of his head.

She didn't like the sound of his wheezing voice or the puffiness around his eyes. "Go change. You might want to take a quick shower."

"We have to find Chris," he said stubbornly.

Marly was already pulling fresh clothing from her dresser. "We will." She refused to believe anything else. How far could the boy have gone? And why?

Sam gave a terse nod and headed across the hall. Her hands trembled as she pulled on underwear and clean jeans. How did Sam know Chris was missing, and what on earth was he doing covered in hay at a quarter after five in the morning?

Marly stuffed her feet into a pair of worn work boots and headed for Chris's room. As Sam had said, Chris's bed was empty. Jerome, however, stirred.

"Go back to sleep," she told him quietly.

Jerome sat up, rubbing his eyes. "Did Sam find Chris?"

She heard the shower running in the connecting bathroom. "Not yet."

"I can help."

"If we don't find him in a few minutes, I'll need everyone's help. For now, you stay put so you don't get lost, too, okay?"

"Okay."

Why had Chris left the house? None of the answers that sprang to her mind were reassuring. Why was Sam covered in hay? How could a cowboy be allergic to hay?

She checked the other rooms quickly, carefully, while questions multiplied in her head. Everyone else was still asleep. There was no sign of Chris.

Sam had figured prominently in her dreams. Racy, heart-thumping dreams, most unlike her subconscious. She would not think of those dreams, and she'd be thankful that no one else could know about them.

She heard him sneezing as soon as she entered his bedroom. The shower had stopped, and the bathroom door was ajar.

Nodding in satisfaction, she called out. "Sam? You okay?"

"Yes." He sneezed. "I'll be right out."

"I left the epinephrine on my bed, if you think you need it. Chris isn't anywhere up here. I'm going downstairs to wake Emma."

She thought he responded, but she wasn't sure. The image of that powerful chest sprinkled with water droplets was as out of place as her dreams had been. Was this why men thought widows and divorcées were fair game? Why was she even thinking about Sam right now?

"Because you don't want to think about why Chris is missing. Get hold of yourself."

She roused Emma and finished searching the downstairs. Sam entered the kitchen. He was dressed in fresh clothing. His hair was wet and his eyes were swollen slits in his face, but he looked marginally better, and she resisted an impulse to touch him.

"Anything?" Sam asked.

"The front door is unlocked. Did you do that?"

"No. It was open when I came downstairs."

"I locked it last night," she stated with a sinking feeling. "That means Chris left under his own power. Doesn't it?"

"Depends. Who else has keys to the house?"

"Carter. My parents." She thought a moment. "My ex-husband. Tell me what happened."

"Jerome woke me and said Chris was gone. I checked around, found the front door unlocked and checked the barn."

"That was a good thought."

"Yeah. I hope it isn't the route the kid took. I wasn't the only one in the barn."

Cold iced her stomach at his tone. "What do you mean?"

"Someone attacked me with the pulley."

Marly focused on his face. She heard the words, but her mind didn't want to accept them. "Who?"

"Well, it wasn't Chris. Someone was in the loft. An adult." He paused, as though trying to assess his next words. "I never got a look at the person. He tried to nail me with the hook. When that missed, he buried me under a pile of hay."

"That's crazy."

"It gets worse," he assured her. "Whoever it was took a young goat up there. He planned to hang it from the pulley."

"*What?*" The world narrowed to this man and his outrageous tale. Fury soared through her at the horrible image his words created. Her mouth went dry with fear. "Why would anyone—?" She couldn't force the rest of the words out.

"There's a note. It says next time it will be a real kid."

The words landed like a blow.

This is your last warning. Get rid of those kids before there's trouble.

That was what the caller had told her the last time. She took an involuntary step backward and came up against the cold metal of the stove. Sam reached out a hand and steadied her.

Bile rose in her throat. Sam sneezed, but that didn't negate his own anger, clearly expressed in the harsh planes of his face.

"I'm going to the bunkhouse and wake Carter. We need to find Chris."

"You don't think he saw the person—?" She couldn't finish that sentence either.

"It's possible. I don't know where he went or what he might have seen, but we don't want to delay the search any longer."

She straightened up. "You're right. I'll meet you outside."

"Why don't you stay here until Carter and I search the barn?"

"Like hell."

"Marly, if there's an intruder on the grounds, the last thing we want is him getting inside the house."

"Damn." She hated his logic, because he was right.

"I'll let you know what we find."

Numb, she watched him open the back door and hurry across the deck. Her neighbors to the east raised goats. One of the females had just had twins. She didn't know why that thought had ambushed her, but she wanted to gag. She wanted to scream. Her fingers curled into tight fists. A fit of hysterics would have gone nicely about now. Too bad she wasn't the type to have them. Fortunately, neither was Emma.

Her friend stepped into the kitchen, belting a long housecoat. "Basement?" she asked.

"You're right. I didn't check."

Time flew by in a haze of fear. Chris was not inside the house. Nor did the men, roused from their beds, find any sign of Chris or an intruder.

Marly kept hoping Chris was simply hiding somewhere she hadn't thought to look. When she spotted Sam and Carter in a heated argument outside in the yard, she hurried to join them. They stopped talking as she approached.

"Go back to the house," Carter ordered.

His tone gave her the edge she needed. "Have you forgotten which one of us is in charge around here, Carter?"

The tall man paled, running blunt fingers through his hatless hair. "Look, I'm sorry—"

Sam intervened. "You should call the police, Marly."

So that was what they'd been arguing about. She looked at Sam's ravaged face, puffy almost beyond recognition.

"You should stay out of that barn, Sam."

He ignored her comment. "There's no sign of Chris."

Marly shut her eyes, while her heart pounded out a staccato. "You think he's been kidnapped? By the person who left that note?"

"No."

"How the devil can you say that?" Carter demanded.

"There are no tire tracks, and I didn't hear a car or a horse leaving," Sam said quietly. "Whoever was in that loft left in a hurry after he pushed those hay bales over on me. I'm more concerned that Chris may have seen what happened and ran away to hide. We need to call the police. It's unfortunate Carter disturbed the evidence.''

"Damn it, Moore. I told you to let me handle things. We don't need the goddamn cops." Carter's fists bunched at his side. Sam faced him in silence.

Marly stepped between them. "Stop it. Did you put all the horses outside?"

"Yes," Carter snarled. "They're all accounted for. There's no one hiding in any of the stalls. Look, Marly, you know the cops aren't going to care about a goat. They've done nothing but give us grief since last summer. What good is calling them going to do?"

"There's a little boy missing, Carter," Sam stated quietly. "They'll care."

"A damn juvenile delinquent. How much do you think they'll—"

"I said, stop it. Both of you."

Carter's face was ruddy with anger, while Sam looked calm and relaxed. Marly knew he wasn't. She could almost hear him blaming himself for Chris's disappearance. She had put him in charge of the boys—even asked him if he was a sound sleeper.

"It isn't your fault, Sam," she told him. "We'll find Chris. Officer Porterfield said he'd be here at noon."

Sam started visibly, but Carter erupted before she could do more than wonder at Sam's reaction.

"That's all we need. Why the hell is that pompous, fat—?" He stopped when he saw Marly's expression. "Well, why *is* he coming out here now? It's not time for his inspection."

Marly sighed. "He called last night, while I was at dinner. He asked if he could drop by today because he's going out of town on vacation or something. I told him that was fine."

Carter started to curse until he saw her glare.

"I want to see the note," she said.

"What for?" Carter demanded. "It's ugly, Marly. Cutout letters on cheap white paper."

"I want to see it."

"We released the harness," Carter continued. "The goat is downstairs in one of the stalls right now."

"The note, Carter."

Carter pursed his lips, glared at Sam and dug into the pocket of his jacket. He pulled forth a crumpled sheet of paper.

"You shouldn't have touched this," she told him, and caught Sam's nod of agreement.

"What the hell difference does it make?"

"They might have been able to get fingerprints from it," Sam stated.

Carter muttered something Marly didn't catch.

"I'm pretty sure the goat belongs to the Linningtons," she told them. "I'll have to call."

She unfolded the note and stared at the jumble of letters. It was crude. Dirty. Evil. She stepped back before Carter could lay his hand on her shoulder and looked up at the barn. "I'm going inside."

"Why? It's just a goat."

"In my barn," she told him, folding the note and thrusting it into her hip pocket.

"Chris isn't in there, Marly," Sam stated.

"You don't mind if I have a look around, do you, Sam?" He shrugged and started to follow her inside. She rounded on him. "Stay out here, or you *will* need the epinephrine."

"I'll be fine," he told her.

"As long as you wait here. Both of you." She glared at both men. "I'll be right out."

Inside the barn, she closed her eyes and prayed she wouldn't vomit from the emotions roiling in her stomach. The entire sequence of events was threatening to swamp her. When she opened her eyes, the first thing she saw was Jake watching her intently from an empty stall.

"What are you doing in there?" she demanded, shaken in spite of herself.

"Carter said I was to keep watch and not let no one disturb anything."

"Where's the goat?"

Almost gleefully, he pointed toward a stall. "Cute little feller, ain't he?"

Marly turned away without replying. She would have to call the people who owned the goat and let them know. The mama goat was a family pet, and this little guy wasn't old enough to have been weaned. It had folded its legs, and was sitting in a pile of hay, looking lost and miserable. The couple he belonged to owned a working acreage. They were among the few neighbors she had who weren't angry about her decision to establish the youth program.

At least they hadn't been angry until now.

"You're sure Chris isn't hiding in here somewhere?"

"Yep. He ain't in here."

She turned to find Carter waiting just inside the barn door. "Are you okay, Marly?"

"I'm fine. Where's Sam?"

At the mention of the other man, his face hardened. "He went back to the house to talk to the kids."

Carter grabbed her by the arm to prevent her walking away. Marly stood still, fighting an urge to shrug away from that touch. When had Carter started acting so possessive?

"What do you know about this Moore fellow?"

"What do you mean?"

"I mean, is it possible he was sent here deliberately?"

"What are you talking about, Carter?"

"Don't you think it's even mildly curious that he shows up so providentially, and suddenly we have a missing kid and a threatening letter?"

Marly did pull away then. "No, Carter, I don't," she told him flatly. "I think we're lucky Sam is here. He's a caring man who interrupted someone in an act of cruelty to be used as a threat against me."

"Unless he was the one who was going to hang the goat."

Marly blinked at the vehemence behind his words. She shook her head firmly. "He came to my room, Carter. He was covered in hay and sneezing hard enough to pop a blood vessel."

"So?"

"So his only concern is for Chris. Why are you so set on accusing him?"

"I'm not—"

"You are. I trust Sam. He's an honorable man. Even his last employer said so."

"Yeah, right. It was probably a girlfriend or something."

"Carter—"

"Think about it, Marly. A cowboy who's allergic to hay? Who's he trying to fool? More important, why? Unless he's working for the folks down the street. They'd love to see an end to your youth camp. You know that. Look at Johnny D."

Marly strove for control. There was an element of truth to what Carter was saying.

"I've worked for you for years now, Marly. You know I care about you, about this place." His eyes bored into hers with fevered intensity. "Maybe Sam is legit. I'm just saying you should be careful here. We don't know anything about him. He's a self-proclaimed drifter, and the timing is just too coincidental."

Carter was right. She did need to be careful. Hadn't she already decided Sam was not what he seemed?

"We need to hold off calling the cops," Carter insisted. "Chris is around here someplace. After all, how far could he go? Let's try to find him before Porterfield gets here. I'll get Jake to take the goat back, and we won't mention the incident to anyone until we have to."

"What if the two things are connected? What if whoever stole the goat has Chris?"

His head swayed from side to side. "I don't believe it. Even Sam claims there was only one person up there besides himself. We'll find Chris. I promise."

Carter was a good man, too. He had worked for her a long time now, and his concern for her was real. He had always had her best interests at heart. Maybe he'd become a bit proprietary, but some of that was her fault. She'd relied too heavily on him when her marriage started to fall apart. He was a terrific trainer, and his ideas had benefited the farm. If he had other ideas about him and her, she'd just have to set him straight in no uncertain terms.

"Okay. We'll hold off calling the police a little longer. But if we haven't found Chris by the time Officer Porterfield gets here—"

"We will. I'll get the men to saddle up. We'll start a search grid right away."

Marly nodded and headed for the house. A subdued group of youngsters were just getting up from the breakfast table. No one had done much eating. Five pair of eyes looked up as she entered the room.

She tried to smile, but couldn't make her lips comply.

Emma hovered in the doorway, watching. "Are you guys all finished?"

Heads bobbed in response.

"We're gonna help search now," Jerome announced.

Marly blinked. "Ah, I don't—"

"The boys and I have worked out a plan."

She whirled to find Sam filling the doorway behind her. He was still suffering from the effects of his bout with the hay, but there was a look of grim determination on his face.

"I don't think—"

"Who better to find a kid than another kid? Why don't you grab something to eat and join us? The boys gave me a list of places that they'd hide if it was them. We'll split the list."

There was a calm determination about him that inspired confidence, despite her misgivings. Maybe he wasn't who or what he claimed, but she had no doubt he would do his damnedest to find Chris. And she didn't believe for a minute that he'd had anything to do with the goat.

"I'll eat later," she told him. "Let me see the list." She caught Emma nodding encouragingly. Sam handed her the paper. Her eyes scanned the places the kids had come up with, and a cold chill snaked its way up her spine. "My God."

"What is it?"

"This rock formation they're talking about? It's the site of the old well. My husband hauled all those boulders to cover the opening when the well went dry."

"Chris liked to play there," Jerome piped up. "We played superheroes."

Her fear was mirrored in Sam's eyes. The rock formation was down past the training ring. She had already told the boys they weren't allowed to play there. The counselor had scolded them twice before for going down there. What could be more inviting than a pile of forbidden rocks? And what could be more dangerous than a hidden well below them?

Chapter Five

"If you don't mind my asking, why didn't you fill in the well, instead of covering it over with rocks?"

There was genuine curiosity behind Sam's question and, amazingly, not a trace of censure. They had decided to check the well together before splitting up. The boys raced ahead, having been cautioned not to get too close. They were excited to be a part of things, and Sam had been right to include them in the search for Chris, she realized.

"He did fill in some of it," Marly explained, "but it was a deep well, and frankly, we didn't have the money to do it right. When one of the rocks jammed partway down, my husband just covered the opening with some bigger ones." She heard the resignation in her voice, but she was tired of trying to explain her ex-husband's actions to people. "Do you think Chris is in there?"

"I don't know, but the kids seem to think it was one of his favorite places to go, besides the hayloft, and we know he isn't up there."

"But he might have been."

Sam made no response. Nor did she expect one. They both knew the barn was the logical place for the boy to hide.

The kids reached the outcropping and began calling Chris. Sam circled the pile of boulders thoughtfully. It was Jerome who discovered the almost hidden opening.

"It's too small," Marly said patiently.

"No, it ain't. See?"

Before she could stop him, he rushed over and wiggled into the narrow aperture. Marly lunged forward, reaching inside to grab his feet just as Jerome gave a yelp of surprise.

"Sam!"

"Right here, Marly. Don't let him go. I've got you."

She felt his strong hands on her legs.

"Can you pull him back?" he asked.

"I think so."

She began to pull, aware of Sam's strength anchoring her. After a moment, Jerome wriggled to help. In seconds he was free, his chocolate eyes wide open in shock.

"There's a hole in there!" he exclaimed.

"I know. That's the well." She hugged him close, thankful he was all right.

"I almost fell down."

"But you didn't," she told him, sending up another prayer of thanks.

"Do you think Chris did?" one of the other boys asked.

"Only one way to find out," Sam said grimly.

"No!"

He eyed her.

"You won't fit," Marly told him. "I'll do it."

"Marly—"

"Hold my legs like you did before. I brought a flashlight." His startled look almost made her smile. "Emma gave it to me."

"Remind me to kiss her later."

"Not a chance. She's already smitten with you."

"I'll remember that."

Marly turned on her stomach and inched toward the narrow opening. This was the last thing she wanted to be doing. There were probably snakes in there.

Sam's hands held firm on her ankles. Marly extended the flashlight and squirmed forward carefully. For a moment, she thought her hips were too wide to clear the aperture, but with a little painful contorting, she made it.

About four feet from the mouth, the ground suddenly fell away. Even though she was expecting it, the instant appearance of the hole came as a surprise to her. She shone the light down inside, and her breath spilled out on a gasp. He looked like a small pile of rags caught in the beam of her light. He didn't move.

"Chris?" Her voice cracked, and she swallowed hard. "Chris? Can you hear me?"

There was no sound, no sign of any movement.

"Christopher, you answer me!"

There was the slightest stirring, or was that only her wistful imagination?

"Marly?" Sam's rough voice was accompanied by a tugging on her legs. Reluctantly she allowed him to pull her back. She twisted around as soon as her head was free.

"He's in there, Sam. About eight to ten feet down. I think he's alive."

Sam turned to the children. "Mickey, you and Donald run back to the house. Tell Emma to call 911." The two boys sprinted away.

"Jerome, you and the other boys go over to the bunkhouse," he continued. "See if any of the men are still there. If they aren't, come straight back here. Don't go in the barn, understand? If you see any of the men, tell them to bring ropes. Got it?" The other three took off across the meadow.

"Sam, I could climb down there. If I go feetfirst—"

"No."

"It isn't that far down."

"No."

"But—"

"Marly, we don't need two victims. This pile of rocks doesn't look stable to me. What if the whole thing shifts? We aren't going to take chances. What equipment did your husband use to pile them here in the first place?"

"I'm not sure. I wasn't here when he did it."

"We'll wait for help."

"But Chris—"

"Will be fine. Kids are resilient."

And she knew then that he was saying the words aloud in an effort to make them true. She reached out and encircled his neck, while a tear tracked its way down her face. After a momentary hesitation, Sam hugged her in return, rocking her silently against his broad chest.

"I'm scared," she whispered.

"Me too." Abruptly he pulled free, stood up and began to circle the pile of rocks again.

Marly wiped at her eyes. "What are you doing?"

Sam tipped his battered Stetson back on his forehead and continued to frown. "Trying to find a better way in."

"You mean a bigger hole, don't you?"

Sam didn't argue. Carter and the rest of the men were pelting across the field toward them, followed by the children. Tersely Sam explained the situation to the men.

"What do you propose?" Carter snapped.

"Well, either we wait for the professionals, or one of us has to go in feetfirst and bring the boy out."

"I told you I'd do that," Marly stated.

"I can do it," Jake said.

Sam regarded the small man thoughtfully. "What do you know about first aid?"

"I can stick a bandage on."

"While I'm fully trained and certified in first aid and CPR," Marly said firmly. "We'll need a backboard. There's one in the barn. Keefer, run and get it right away, please."

She looked at the anxious children and once again sent them running for blankets, water, and the walkie-talkies. As the boys ran back toward the house, she looked at Sam. His brown eyes gleamed in troubled approval before he turned toward her foreman.

"Carter, let's rig up a system with the ropes. Have you got more?"

"Yeah," he agreed. "Jake?"

"On my way."

It seemed an eternity before Sam had things set up enough to suit him. Marly noticed that everyone, including Carter, deferred to him in this. She was harnessed into a set of ropes and, when Sam gave the word, began to inch her way backward though the hole. They had decided not to send the backboard down until she was ready. Sam wasn't sure it would fit through the opening.

Marly was surprised to find the drop deeper than she had thought. It was easily ten feet down. The men lowered her slowly until she found herself standing on the large boulder wedged precariously over the rest of the well. Chris lay at her feet.

A shifting noise gave her a bad moment, wondering if the rock would hold under their combined weight. It felt decidedly unstable. Then she bent over Chris, who was curled in a fetal position. His eyes fluttered open as she ran exploratory fingers over his body.

"Marly?"

"Don't move, Chris. Where are you hurt?"

"My head. I tried to climb out, but I fell. I can't get out."

"Okay, don't worry. We'll get you out in a minute. Does your neck hurt?"

"No. Just my head."

She felt along the back of his head and found an enormous raised area where he'd struck it. There was no sign of bleeding, but the pupil of one eye was slightly larger than the other one, so she was pretty sure he had a concussion.

"How about your back?"

"It doesn't hurt. My knee hurts."

His knee was scraped. There was no sign of swelling. Marly breathed a sigh of relief.

"It's cold down here."

He was right about that. She saw his body shiver and unwrapped the impossibly lightweight camping blanket from her kit and draped it over him. Then she picked up the walkie-talkie. Sam answered at once.

"He's conscious and alert. There's a blow to the back of his head, but no obvious breaks I can determine. Is the rescue squad there yet?"

"No. I sent Keefer to call again."

Without warning, the rock beneath her feet shifted. Marly's heart leaped into her throat. "Sam?"

"Marly? What's wrong?"

His voice crackled sharply over the tinny speaker. She tried to keep her own voice calm, in an effort to match his tone, not wanting to scare Chris any further. "We can't wait for the rescue squad."

"What's wrong, Marly?" Sam's voice was a strong, quiet lifeline. She took a steadying breath.

"The rock isn't stable. I think it might be slipping. We have to bring him up now. See if the backboard fits."

There was a moment of silence in which she could picture him tipping back his hat and cursing. After a moment, his voice filled the eerie cave.

"Marly? It's a definite no for the backboard."

The sound of dirt shifting pumped up her heart.

"We can't wait, Sam."

"Okay," he said calmly. "What do you want to do?"

"I'm going to tie my lines around Chris so you can pull him out."

"Negative." The word whipped out at her. "Keep the lines around yourself in case the rock goes, Marly. I'll send Jake to the lip to drop a second set of lines over. Use them to tie around Chris the way I did around you."

Her breath jammed in her throat as the slipping sensation came again.

"Marly? Did you copy?"

Her finger shook as she depressed the call button. "I heard you Sam, but hurry. I don't think we have much time."

"Affirmative." His tone was grim, but he smoothed it as he added, "Hang in there, boss."

The whole thing reminded her of a movie in which a plane was going down in flames and the pilot was calmly reporting the situation. Knowing Sam was listening to her was foolishly reassuring, somehow.

"Chris?"

At the sound of her voice, the boy opened his eyes but they were glazed. Was he getting worse?

"Listen, sweetie, we're going to get you out of here, but you have to help me, okay?"

"'Kay."

There was a noise above them, and dirt rained down on her head.

"Marly?"

It was Jake's voice. His face was hidden behind the flashlight he was shining down on her.

"Right here, Jake."

"Okay. I'm gonna come down and—"

"No! The rock won't hold any more weight. Stay where you are, Jake!"

"Okay, okay, take it easy. Can the boy climb?"

She shone her own light down on him. "I don't think so."

"Then you'll have to pass him up to me. I'm gonna lower the other ropes Sam gave me. Tie them around the kid the way Sam did to you, and try to pass him to me. I'll grab him and pull him free."

"Okay."

The ropes descended in a shower of dirt. Marly thought the rock shifted again, but she wasn't sure, with all the dirt falling from above. Her hands were numb with fear. When she grabbed for the end of the rope, a grating noise sounded from beneath her feet.

"Gawd," Jake whispered. "Be careful, boss."

Her mouth was too dry for her to respond. She nodded and bent to tie the line around Chris. He was limp, and only partly conscious. That scared her even more.

"Chris!" His eyes fluttered open. "Listen to me. Hold on to this rope, okay? Can you do that?"

He blinked and mumbled something that might have been assent. She took his icy hands and placed them on the rope. "Jake, he's more unconscious than not. I don't think he's going to be much help."

"You sure you don't want me to come down?"

"Positive." Even as she said the word, she could hear the dirt continuing to shift around her. "I'm going to tell Sam to start pulling. You'll have to reach for Chris, but I'll try to guide him upward as far as I can."

"Okay."

She flicked the switch on the walkie-talkie. "Sam?"

"Right here, Marly. What's going on?"

"Chris is almost unconscious, and this rock is definitely going. I've tied the lines around him like you showed me. You'd better start pulling. Slowly. He's not going to be much help."

"Understood."

Marly clipped the walkie-talkie to her waistband. "Okay, Jake. Here he comes."

She strained to lift the eighty pounds or more of essentially dead weight over her head, expecting that at any moment the bottom would fall out of her world, literally. The dirt continued to shift, but the rock held.

Chris helped more than she'd thought he could as they inched him upward. Finally, Jake's hands gripped him. In minutes both of them were out of sight and she was left shaking in reaction, with only a first-aid kit and a flashlight at her feet.

"Marly? We've got him," Sam's voice said from the small box at her waist. "You ready?"

"In a second." She replaced the walkie-talkie at her waist and bent to collect the other items. The rock suddenly gave way. A scream tore from her lungs as she found herself plunging downward, only to suddenly slam against a dirt wall as the ropes brought her up short.

The flashlight winked out. Empty blackness surrounded her as she dangled in midair.

"Marly! Marly, damn it, answer me!"

She hung from the ropes, too terrified to let go. There was a scuffling sound overhead, and dirt sprinkled her again. But there was light. Blessed light. It seemed a long way up this time.

"Marly? You all right?" Jake asked.

It took her two tries to get her voice to cooperate. "Yes." It sounded scratchy, hoarse with the terror that was closing in on her mind. She forced herself to speak calmly. "Can you get me out?"

The ropes dug into her skin.

"Hang on, I'll be right back."

"No! Don't go!"

But Jake had already disappeared from sight. Seconds later, Sam's static-filled voice began to speak. "Take it easy, Marly. Don't panic on us now. We've got you. The ropes are strong. We won't let you fall."

She swallowed back the terror, wishing she could respond, but still too scared to let go of the ropes.

"Listen to me, Marly," Sam continued. "I'm going to talk you up the whole way, okay? Don't try to respond, just listen to me and do as I say."

"Like I have a choice," she muttered shakily.

"We're going to start pulling. I want you to use your feet and your hands to help us. Use the sides for leverage."

Marly gave an involuntary scream as the ropes began to pull against her weight.

"Marly? You okay?"

Jake's voice, and the blessed light that seemed so far away.

"Yes. It just scared me."

"Okay. Sam says we'll get you out faster if I'm outside, outta the way."

She tried to slow her breathing. "Okay. But can you leave the light?"

"Sure thing. Sam'll have you out in a jiffy."

"Good. Tell him to hurry. I wasn't cut out to dangle over a pit."

Jake chuckled. "I'll tell 'im."

Moments later, Sam's slow voice filled her ears again.

"Okay, boss, Jake says you're in a hurry."

The ropes jerked. This time she managed not to scream.

"But we aren't going to do it fast, Marly. We're going to go slow. It's always better that way, don't you think?" His voice was low, and pitched for seduction.

"Skip the innuendos and get me out of here, Moore." But, of course, he couldn't hear her unless she depressed the send button, and he was already talking, in a slow, easy drawl that still managed to sound like an invitation to bed, even over a crackling walkie-talkie.

"Come on, baby, plant your feet. That's it, darlin' don't make me do all the work. It's better when both of us cooperate, don't you think?"

"I'll show you cooperate," she muttered, but she was using one of her hands and both of her feet in an effort to help.

"We'll slide you right on out of that hole and into my waitin' arms, darlin'."

"In your dreams, cowboy." Even if it did sound like heaven.

"That's it, nice an' easy. Keep comin', sweetheart. I've got you."

"You'd better, or you're fired." But she actually smiled. The light was growing brighter, nearer. She dug in with renewed effort.

"Now you're comin'. A little more, darlin'. You're almost there."

Suddenly, the ropes jerked and she slipped downward almost a foot. She heard Sam's curse, but she didn't have time to scream. Her heart was lodged against the back of her throat.

She could hear shouts and disjointed noises, but mostly she heard Sam expel a harsh breath. "I've got her," he panted. "Get in front of me and pull, damn it."

Marly clawed for a handhold in the dirt before her. Something had gone wrong with the ropes. She didn't need Sam to tell her that.

"On three," Sam said. "Pull!"

She jerked upward. No longer was there a smooth, slow ride. They pulled on Sam's command. She gripped the ropes and began to climb. In minutes, her fingers were scrabbling for the top. She gouged for a handhold on the lip of the well and got a faceful of dirt for her efforts. But the men yanked, and she was suddenly over the top and they were dragging her toward blessed daylight.

Carter's arms reached for her wrists. He tugged her forward. Her hips scraped against the rocks, and then she was outside and he was pulling her to her feet. He hugged her tightly to his body, saying something, but she only had eyes for the man sitting in the dirt against a rock, a bloody rope in his hand.

She struggled free of Carter and came to stand above

her cowboy. His hat was shoved way back. Streaks of dirt and sweat ran down his face, but she had never seen anyone more handsome in all her life. The look in his brown eyes lifted her heart.

"Well, cowboy," she said, breathing hard. "Was it good for you, too?"

His astonished expression gave way to a shout of laughter, and he climbed to his feet to reach for her.

A man in an impeccable white shirt and navy trousers intercepted their embrace. The paramedics had arrived.

"Ms. Kramer, come on over here and let us check you out."

She shot Sam a look of frustration, but he didn't notice.

"Marly," Carter's rough voice said in her ear, "they want to know if you're going to ride along with Chris."

"Yes, of course. I just need to get my purse."

Jerome stepped forward and handed it to her. "Emma told me to bring it. Is Chris gonna be okay?"

"I hope so, sweetie." She ignored the waiting paramedic and gave the boy a hug.

"You need to look at Sam's hands," she told the paramedic as she rose. The frayed rope near her feet told the story. When it started to go, only Sam had kept her from falling.

Sam met her eyes. She strode forward, wanting nothing more than to throw her arms around his neck and kiss him senseless. Mindful of the children and the others clustered around, she didn't give in to her wants, but she saw an answering hunger for just a moment in the heat that blazed from his eyes.

"Hey, now," he whispered. "You okay?"

"Thanks to you."

"And Carter and Jake and Keefer and—"

She stepped forward then, and brushed her lips across his dusty cheek. Her lips didn't linger, but the hoots and catcalls of the watching children brought color to her own cheeks and fired the heat of his look. He made no move to touch her.

"Thanks, Sam." She turned to Carter then, shaken by emotions she couldn't have named. "You'll need to wait here for Porterfield. Then I'd appreciate it if you'd bring him along to the hospital."

There was a dark look of anger on Carter's face. "Okay."

Marly climbed into the back of the ambulance without assistance. She watched Sam watching her until they were out of sight.

SAM WASHED his hands again, wincing as the soap bit into the rope burns and small cuts. If he'd thought he ached yesterday, after that little bit of riding and post-hole-digging, he should have waited. His shoulders burned with the strain of pulling Marly and Chris out of the pit. Not that the others hadn't helped. Every one of the men had pulled his weight, literally. They were a good crew.

He swallowed two more antihistamines and pulled on his last pair of clean jeans. He was going to have to do some laundry or get into town to buy more clothes. He thought about the slim contents of his wallet and knew he'd have to wash the clothes, even if it meant putting them in the bathroom sink.

He opened the door to his room and paused. Voices wafted up the stairs. Familiar voices. Bill Porterfield had arrived. Sam tossed the clothing on the bed and strained to hear what was being said. The voices stopped, and heavy feet started coming up the stairs. He shut the door, slipped his gun from his boot and stepped into the bathroom.

Porterfield wore glasses, so Sam turned on the hot water in the shower and waited. He heard the tap on his bedroom door, and Carter Delancy's voice called out. Carter didn't wear glasses, but Sam wasn't worried about being seen by him.

"Out in a minute!" he shouted. He waited, gun in hand, for the bathroom knob to turn. It didn't.

"I'm going into town to get Marly," Carter yelled. "Keep the kids out of trouble until I get back. Emma'll watch them until you're done."

"I'll be right out," he promised. As soon as they were gone.

He waited another three minutes before he turned off the shower and opened the door. One of the windows in his room overlooked the front of the house. Careful to stay out of direct line of sight, Sam approached and peered outside. Bill Porterfield's substantial girth was unmistakable as he fit himself behind the wheel of his familiar green sedan. Carter drove Marly's truck. Sam waited until they both pulled out of the yard before he descended the staircase.

He was almost instantly surrounded by small bodies. "Sam, can we go riding now? Emma said we had to wait for you."

"Yeah, Sam, there's nothing to do."

Emma was watching from the shadows at the end of the hall. With Chris gone, he had planned to disappear as soon as Porterfield left, but seeing the five hopeful expressions, he groaned inwardly. It might be better after all to stay and work with the boys for a while first. Maybe he could still find a way to get to Chris.

Sam could be pretty sure Bill and Carter wouldn't be

coming back from the hospital for at least a couple of hours. In fact, if he could duck Bill's visit completely, he might not have to leave right away.

"Okay. Get your riding boots, and let's go over to the training ring."

"Aw, do we still have to walk in circles like babies?"

"Well, now, that all depends on how well you can follow orders, doesn't it?"

Ten minutes later, Sam had five pairs of attentive eyes on him as he demonstrated how to saddle a horse. The mare he'd selected was docile to the point of being completely disinterested in the entire proceedings. The gelding was a little livelier, but settled down nicely under Sam's soothing tone. As the afternoon sun grew steadily hotter, he had the boys take turns mounting and riding around the training ring.

"I need to see how well you guys can manage a horse," he told them.

Sam smiled at their perceptive questions. While they fooled around some outside the ring, none of them acted foolish on top of the horses, and all of them took corrections surprisingly well.

"Okay. Tomorrow, we'll take six horses and try one of the pastures."

"How come we can't do it today?" Zeke wanted to know.

"Because I'm too sore to ride with you guys today," he told them honestly.

"Oh." No one argued after that.

He had two of the boys unsaddle the animals, and let one boy help him hold the horses while the others learned to use a currycomb.

"Tomorrow we'll ask Marly for the best trail to take, okay?"

There were shouts of pleasure, and they headed back to the main house in a jubilant mood. Emma had fresh-baked cookies and pitchers of lemonade and milk sitting on the front porch. He left the boys digging into the snack and went up to his room to get the laundry and take another antihistamine tablet. The pile of clothing had disappeared from his bed. Emma, no doubt.

Returning downstairs, he located her in the kitchen. Emma didn't even blink when he requested five relatively sharp knives and six bars of soap. For the next two hours, Sam proceeded to show the boys the fine art of whittling.

"I need my own knife," Jerome grumbled. "This thing ain't no good."

Sam rubbed his coarse head of hair. "It'll do for now. That's a pretty good boat you're working on, Jerome. I'll see what I can do about getting us some better knives later."

"Sam, do you think Chris is gonna die?"

Sam looked down at the boy called Hector and shook his head. "Nope. He's too ornery to die." Sam hoped it was the truth. "But I bet he's gonna wish he hadn't gone outside without permission."

"Why did he?" one of the others wanted to know.

"I expect we'll have to ask him when we see him. Won't we?"

Sam spotted Marly's truck turning into the drive, and he tensed, until he realized it was the only vehicle. He was glad Porterfield hadn't returned with them, but he wondered if that meant good or bad for Chris. They were too far away yet for him to see how many people were inside the cab.

"Hey, that's Marly," one of the boys announced, following the direction of his stare.

"Clean up your shavings," Sam told them. "If we want her to approve of sharper knives, we have to let Marly see you're all responsible adults here, okay?"

The boys set to the task with fervor, if not with perfection. By the time the truck was stopped, they were all standing in the grass, waiting.

She looked exhausted. That was Sam's first thought as Marly stepped down from the cab. Her expression lightened when she caught sight of him and he stood slowly and leaned against the post.

"Chris has a concussion," she said, answering Donald's question. "No, he'll be fine," she told Mickey as they fired questions at her. "They're going to keep him overnight for observation, but he'll be okay. Yes, lots of bruises. Yes, he was very lucky."

Sam felt a presence at his side and turned to see Emma standing there. She smiled with her eyes. "Dinner. Five minutes," she told him, and disappeared back into the house.

"Okay, sports," Sam called out. "Emma says dinner in five minutes. You guys need to go wash up, and give Marly a chance to do the same."

"Why we gotta wash up? We was just playin' with soap."

"Yeah. I want to show Marly what I made."

As the entire procession headed for the porch and the small soap carvings, Carter sent Sam a look of pure malice. Before he could react, Carter stalked off without a word to Marly.

What the hell was that all about?

Marly made appropriate comments about the crude carvings, and the boys scurried inside when Sam reminded them that Emma had been baking brownies, as well as cookies, earlier. Marly paused to lean back against the house alongside him.

"Rough day?" he teased.

"Not at all. What makes you ask? I called the family who owned the goat. They were horrified by what happened, but even more indignant at the reason behind the theft."

"You sound surprised." He leaned his hand on the wall near her head and watched her expression. She didn't move away.

"I am surprised. I thought this would make them join the movement to stop my youth program."

She had washed her face and combed her hair, he noticed, but her clothes were badly soiled from her climb into the hole. She looked young. Young and tired and extremely vulnerable.

Her eyes shifted away from his. "I also called a local contractor. He promised to be out this week to fill in the hole."

Sam reached out, even after he told himself not to do it, and brushed back a strand of hair from her face. Her lips parted slightly. They were very provocative lips, he thought once again. "Can you afford it?"

"Can I afford not to?"

Her words were husky and her features softened as she looked at him. She lifted her head a fraction. Sam placed his other hand on the wall beside her head, effectively pinning her between his arms. Her chest rose and fell more quickly. It was also a very provocative chest, he decided. A nice match for her lips.

Slowly, giving her time to push him away, he leaned down and brushed against those lips. They were driving him crazy. *She* was driving him crazy. Marly made a tiny noise and shut her eyes. Her hands rose to circle his neck. It was all the encouragement he needed.

He'd been planning to take things slow. Hell, who was he kidding? He hadn't been planning to kiss her at all. But once he tasted the sweetness of her, he was lost. His hands threaded the thick sheaf of hair at the back of her head, drawing her against him as his mouth roamed her lips, savoring the flavor that was uniquely hers.

His tongue traced the seam of her lips, and she opened for him, touching the tip of her tongue to his. He caught fire. She made another small sound, and he swallowed it as he moved restlessly against her. She pushed herself against him unconsciously. His hands slid down her sides to cup her bottom and draw her even closer. He deepened the kiss, savoring the taste and the texture of her.

"Sam, Emma says come to dinner. Oh, yuck. Kissing."

The dark hair disappeared back inside before Sam could pull away. Marly looked embarrassed and thoroughly kissed. The fingers that she brought to her lips trembled.

"He saw us."

"'Fraid so."

"What should we do?"

"Go inside and eat."

"But—"

"Marly, these are inner-city kids. They've probably seen a lot more than what we were doing on this porch."

"But it's broad daylight."

Sam had to grin, knowing she was so rattled she

didn't know what she was saying. "Yep. Does it get better after dark?"

"Stop that."

"Not a chance. Not if it's going to get better after dark."

"You know what I mean."

He chucked her gently under the chin. "Don't worry, darlin'. You act like nothing happened and so will they."

"But—"

"Come on, I'm suddenly starving. I don't think I ate anything at all today."

SAM MADE UP for his fast at dinner, Marly decided.

"You gonna play with that stuff or eat it?" he asked her, while helping himself to seconds. Only the presence of the boys kept her from sticking her tongue out at him.

He'd been right about the boys, again, darn him. Not one child had said a word about the kiss, even though at least one of them had witnessed it. She could still feel the tingle of his lips, taste the heat of his mouth.

She found Sam watching her, a private smile playing at the corners of his lips. His expression left her powerless to prevent the warmth that stole into her cheeks. She lifted a forkful of something and chewed without tasting.

"This is a great casserole, Emma," Sam said.

"Yes," Marly agreed. "Great." Just great. Divorced less than a year, and she had the hots for the first good-looking man to come her way.

No, that wasn't true. Carter was better-looking, in a classical sense. And Carter had made it plain today that he wanted to be the one to share her bed.

The car ride home from the hospital had been untenable. She'd come within an inch of firing the best trainer she'd ever had. Only how could she have handled their conversation differently? When he started talking about all the changes they would make once they were married, Marly had been stunned. She should have seen it coming. She'd known Carter was attracted, but this...

He hadn't taken the rejection well. He wanted her and he wanted her farm. In that order? Then he'd started raving about Sam. He'd actually demanded she fire him. She could have been more tactful when she put him in his place. Only Carter didn't seem to understand tact. How was it that she knew so little of men? And what was she going to do now?

As soon as the boys were down for the night, she needed to talk to Sam. He was watching her again. There was heat in his smoky look. Heat that reached into her belly and produced an answering response. Marly squirmed, and his eyes crinkled at the corners in knowing amusement.

The telephone rang, snapping her upright in her chair. She couldn't take another one of those calls right now, but maybe it wasn't her nemesis. Maybe it was the hospital. Maybe Chris had taken a turn for the worse.

Marly stood and excused herself, hurrying to the telephone. She was aware of Sam's gaze following her, this time in concern.

"Hello?"

"Get rid of those kids or I will."

Chapter Six

"Who was on the phone, Marly?" Sam filled the doorway of her office.

"Wrong number," she replied quickly.

"From the same person who was going to gift-wrap the goat?"

Marly started, surprised by his perception. He nodded, as if she had answered him. "Did you recognize the voice?"

She shook her head. There was no point in lying now. "It's always hard to hear, as if he muffles his voice somehow."

"But you're sure it's a he?"

Marly started to answer and stopped. "It never occurred to me it could be a woman." Sam continued to watch her steadily. "The voice is too deep, I think."

"Okay. How long have you been getting these calls?"

"Since the boys arrived."

"The police won't help?"

"I don't know. I haven't called them."

"Why not?"

How could she tell him she thought the police were

behind the calls? One policeman, at least. Officer Duncan.

He came around the desk. "May I?"

Without waiting for permission, he lifted the phone and pressed the star key, then 69. "This redials the person who just called. His phone number is automatically recorded—as long as it's within the local calling area—and the police can trace it easily, because now there's a record of the call."

Marly regarded him thoughtfully. "I never thought to do that."

The phone must have been answered after several rings. Even from where she sat, Marly could hear the snapped-out greeting. Her heart thundered in her chest. Sam's face set in hard, angry lines. That anger wasn't reflected when he spoke. "Jake? It's Sam. Marly wants to know if the goat was returned without any problems."

Jake had been making the calls?

She felt stunned. True, she had never been comfortable around the man, but he was a good—and she would have said honest—worker. She should have paid more attention to the fact that he didn't like the kids. It had just never occurred to her that the calls were being made by one of her own men.

"She isn't grousing, Jake, only asking." Sam's tone was mild. It didn't go with his expression. "What about the stock? Yeah. I think that's best, too. No, not tonight. No, we haven't heard anything new. Yeah, I'm sure he will be fine. Right. I'll tell her."

Sam hung up. "You okay?"

She shook her head. "I thought it was Duncan, or one of his neighbors. I never suspected Jake. Why didn't I recognize his voice?"

His hand lay, a soothing comfort against her shoulder. She resisted an impulse to lean against it.

"You said the voice was muffled. Besides, it may not have been Jake."

"He answered the phone."

"The main phone to the bunkhouse, Marly. It rang several times before it was picked up. All that told us was the location of the call—not who made it."

"Jake's the only one of my men who objects to the boys being here."

Sam's expression became thoughtful. "Is he?"

"What does that mean?"

"It means, someone with access to the bunkhouse phone wants to scare you. It means we have to be watchful and alert from now on."

We? Sam was aligning himself with her? Coming from Carter, use of the word *we* would have sounded possessive. From Sam, it merely sounded comforting.

"Jake offered to go down the well after Chris today," she said thoughtfully.

"Yeah. He did. He also asked how Chris was doing."

Marly thought about that. But if not Jake, then who? Duncan wasn't on the premises right now. At least she was pretty sure he wasn't. She couldn't picture Carter making that sort of threat. Why would he? But Lou or Keefer?

"Jake said they left the horses in the pasture for the night," Sam continued.

"Okay, thanks, Sam."

She was intensely aware of his large hand, warming her skin beneath her shirt. She looked up, to find him studying her. His smoldering gaze heated more than her skin. She began to breathe too fast. Erratically.

For a timeless moment, they stared at one another.

Then, as if it were inevitable, he bent down and his
mouth settled over hers. Heat and promises. Marly
stirred in welcome, yet Sam made no move to deepen
the kiss. He pulled back slowly, leaving her to blink
uncertainly.

"Lady, if I didn't have five antsy kids waiting for me
in your dining room, I'd let you thank me properly."

"Ha." Her voice was too shaky—like the rest of her.
She made an effort to gain control, adding a lofty smile
to her words. "I think that's all the thanks you deserve,
cowboy."

"Yeah? Then I guess I'll have to do something else
that's really heroic."

Her heart pounded harder in anticipation.

"Later," he added.

Marly leaned back in her chair and watched him
leave the room with a cocky swagger she was sure he
put on for her benefit. She found herself smiling. It was
the first time she had felt relaxed in days.

"All because he kissed you?" she mused.

No, not just because he'd kissed her, but also because
he'd offered to help. She had confidence in Sam, and,
God help her, for the first time in years, she wanted to
be with a man.

Her smile faded. She had wanted her husband once
too, so what did that say? Be careful what you wish
for?

"I'm smarter now," she told the wranglers in the picture on the wall. "Older. Wiser. This time around, I
don't have to marry the man." She rose from her chair,
circled the desk and strode across the room.

This time around, she could take the few pleasures
to be found in a relationship and send the man packing
when it ended. She lifted the western Remington print

her husband had liked so well and pulled it from the wall. She hated that picture, and it was time to make some changes in her life. This time around, she could walk away without expensive lawyers and crippling emotions.

The thought *should* have left her feeling pleased.

SAM SIGHED as his bedroom door shut with a snick. Marly's kids were going to be the death of him. Getting thrown in jail might almost be preferable to riding herd on five would-be toughs who were still just kids in need of a little direction, some different role models. And wasn't he a great one?

He shrugged off that thought, wondering if there was a spot on his body that didn't ache from directing all that enthusiasm. He touched the sensitive rope burn on his right hand, rolling his shoulders to ease the strain.

Marly had watched from the swing on the porch while he showed the boys a few more self-defense moves tonight. He didn't invite her to participate this time. Touching her was becoming too great a temptation. He couldn't remember the last time a woman had stirred him so much with a simple kiss.

Simple, hell. There was nothing simple about Marly's kiss. It was potent and deadly to a man in his situation.

"I need to call Lee," he muttered.

What he really needed was to get out of here. There was nothing to be accomplished now that Chris was in the hospital. Unless the kid came back to the farm instead of going home, Sam's opportunity to talk to the boy would be better in the city. It was too risky for him to try and visit Chris in the hospital. Each new person who saw Sam was an additional danger. Eventually, someone was bound to recognize him.

Somehow, he needed to get internal affairs to focus on Bill Porterfield. There had to be evidence somewhere, and Sam sure wasn't going to find it sitting on a horse farm in Maryland.

He noticed the neatly folded pile of clothing sitting on his bed. Emma, the good fairy. With a smile, he began to strip. Naked, he padded into the bathroom, turned on the tap and stepped into the shower. The pulsing spray felt wonderful. He let his body absorb the moist heat, feeling it soothe some of his minor aches.

His mind instantly returned to Marly. There was no point in wishing things could be different. She was out-of-bounds. Still, it was hard to keep his mind focused on his own situation, when Marly's troubles were right here to hand. Could she be in danger?

He turned off the shower, troubled by that thought, and toweled himself dry. He was combing his hair in the fogged mirror when he heard a sound from his room. He spun quickly, realizing he hadn't brought his gun into the bathroom with him. It was tucked under his pillow, out of reach. He scanned the room, looking for another weapon. There wasn't one.

A light tap on the bathroom door was immediately followed by Marly's voice. "Sam?"

Relief surged through him, and he wrapped the towel around his waist before throwing open the door.

"What are you doing in here?"

She took a step back, her eyes wide in surprise at his brusk tone. "I thought you might need this." She held out a tube of liniment. It was the same stuff they used on the horses. "It smells foul, I know, but it does a great job on people, too. I've used it myself. I noticed how stiff you were moving when we put the boys down for the night, and I thought…"

She wet her lips. He really wished she hadn't done that. Her cheeks were flushed a pretty pink, and he realized her gaze was now riveted on his chest. A moment later, her gaze slipped lower.

Sam felt an instant, predictable reaction.

He took the tube from her fingers, careful not to touch her. Sam was pretty sure that once he started, he wouldn't be able to stop.

"Thanks. You shouldn't be in here."

The pink deepened. There was hurt in her eyes. It was so tempting to kiss that expression away.

"I didn't—"

"Jerome's on the other side of the bathroom. I'm fairly certain he isn't asleep yet."

She drew herself up in anger. "I didn't come in here for some slap-and-tickle, Sam."

"Well, damn." Relieved by her anger, he leaned casually against the bathroom doorjamb, though what he felt was anything but casual. "There's no one else I'd rather play with."

Her cheeks were cherry red now, and she was breathing hard, but his words had chased away most of the hurt from her expression.

"So I see." She nodded pointedly toward his revealing towel before returning her gaze to his face.

Laughter sputtered forth. Her devil-take-you response was so unexpected it delighted him.

"I'll say good-night then," she told him.

She was almost out the door before he could stop her. As soon as he did it, he realized grabbing her arm had been a mistake. He eased his grip, afraid to mar her skin beneath the soft cotton blouse. She twisted to face him, and he searched her eyes, reading her uncertainty, her vulnerability—and, yes, her desire. The last part made his blood run hot.

"Someday, you'll thank me for being a gentleman."

She tossed her head. "Someday, you'll regret the impulse."

He grinned. "Trust me—I already do."

"Good."

With a low chuckle, he took her mouth. She was soft and sweet, and she responded almost greedily to the probe of his tongue. He swung her all the way around, bringing her yielding body up against him.

Marly wound her arms about his neck, and he told himself to stop. Instead, he slid his fingers up her sides, letting them rest just beneath the fullness of her breasts. She arched against him. That was all the incentive he needed to toss common sense to the winds. His fingers closed over one breast, cupping, then rubbing, then seeking out her nipple.

The soft moan of pleasure that she uttered was like the taste of ambrosia. He pinned her against the wall. Her eyes widened and Sam smiled. "Do you have any idea how sexy you are?"

Her eyes flickered closed in response, and his tongue darted in and out of her hot mouth. Marly made a pleased sound again.

From somewhere down the hall came a thump. Sanity made a belated but instant return. Sam released her, spinning to grab for the door. There was nothing to see in the corridor, but the sound was repeated.

"The kids," he muttered. His hand stabbed at his hair. "Damn it. I'd better go see what they're doing."

"No." She had recovered, as well. "I'll go. You aren't exactly dressed for scolding children. Good night,

Sam." She opened the door and marched down the hall with her head held high.

Was she relieved? Upset?

Or was she as horny as he was?

Her hand pounded on a door. "You have ten seconds and I'm coming in," she warned. Her voice was steady. She never once looked back.

Sam retreated inside his room and closed the door. Picking up the tube of liniment from the floor where he had dropped it, he sagged down onto the bed, next to his clothing. He had to get out of here. This crazy attraction was out of hand. He'd been ready to take her right then and there. What was the matter with him?

Sam lifted the book he had snitched from her den and settled down on the bed in an effort to curb his thoughts. He'd leave in the morning, he decided. There wasn't any other choice.

Pages into the novel, he realized he didn't know who any of the main characters were or even what the plot was about. His mind was on a merry-go-round, spinning uselessly, and Marly was the gold ring, just out of reach. He clicked off the light, determined to catch a quick nap. Sleep proved impossible. His mind refused to put aside thoughts of the woman across the hall. What would her hair feel like against his chest?

"Damn it." Sam sat up and stared around his dark bedroom. He was wanted in connection with a homicide. He didn't have time to be thinking about anything else. Getting information was critical. Surely Lee would have something for him by now. Sam leaned back against the headboard, watching the digital clock flip numerals and listening to the sounds of the house settling for the night.

At 1:10, he pulled on his jeans. Barefoot, he headed

downstairs to the den. Familiar with the layout, Sam went right to the desk and the telephone. He dialed Lee's number in the darkness and thought about the risk he was taking. It was an even bigger risk tonight. If Lee had told George, or anyone, about his earlier call, the line was sure to be tapped.

"Have to trust somebody," he muttered as the phone ran unanswered in his ear. Besides, he was pretty sure Lee wouldn't turn him in. "Come on, partner, wake up." But the phone simply continued to ring.

"Damn." He replaced the receiver and stared at the wall. Lee might be working tonight. Sam would have to wait and call him again in a few hours. Or he could call the captain. The more he thought about it, the better the idea seemed. Except that George was married. Cassandra wouldn't take kindly to a call at this hour, and for sure she'd want to know who it was. It had been pretty apparent to him that George and his wife were having problems lately. The last thing he wanted to do was add to them. No, he couldn't call George.

Unsettled, he stood and walked over to the window. The moon darted in and out between low scudding clouds, casting eerie shadows over the lawn. Sam spotted one of the horses moving restlessly in the paddock area next to the barn. That was odd. Jake had told him they turned the horses out into the field for the night.

He stared out over the porch. Nothing moved, other than an occasional firefly, but he felt a building sense of unease he couldn't quite shrug off. It was probably the approaching storm. Marly wouldn't like the horses being outside if the weather turned nasty. Maybe he should rouse Carter. The two of them could stable the animals quickly.

A flicker of light caught his attention. His eyes strove

to focus on the barn. There was light coming from the loft. Someone was moving around in there. Damn. He'd meant to check that out earlier, but he'd been side-tracked by the kids.

He raced for the stairs. Having grown up around horses, Sam knew better than to enter a barn in his bare feet. Besides, he needed his gun. In his room, he grabbed his boots from beside the bed and stuffed his feet inside. He had just reached for his gun when light poured into the hall and a shadow filled his open doorway.

"Oh!"

Sam didn't have to wonder why Marly had gasped. He shoved the offending gun down in his boot and tugged on his shirt. She was backlit in his doorway by the light spilling from her room. Her long, silky hair tumbled about her shoulders. That image was going to haunt his dreams tonight. If he ever got to sleep, that is.

"Sam, what are you doing? I heard you run upstairs."

So she hadn't been able to sleep, either. Any other time, he would have been pleased by that notion. Not now. "There's someone in the barn."

"What? Who?"

"That's what I'm going to find out. Stay here."

"Don't tell me what to do," she snapped back.

He grabbed her shoulders. "After what happened last night, you stay here. Someone planned to hang a goat. No telling what he's hanging right now."

She looked stunned. He released her shoulders and started for the steps.

"Where did you get the gun?"

Sam didn't bother to answer her question. "Wait

right there. If I'm not back inside of ten minutes, call
the police.''

"No. Wait, Sam."

He was already halfway down the stairs. It was still
hot outside, but a breeze tumbled past, pushing clouds
across the night sky. Sam could almost feel the approaching rain. He took time to scan his surroundings.
Lightning flashed in the distance. A car sat parked at
the far end of the driveway. It was off to one side, and
completely dark, partially hidden beneath a cluster of
dogwoods.

He withdrew the gun. Whoever went with that car
was probably inside the barn. He cursed the fact that
there was no cover of any sort between the house and
the other building. All the person inside had to do was
look out and Sam would be spotted before he got anywhere near the barn door. He could only hope the person was too busy to look.

The light coming from the loft was brighter now. Too
bright. Sam caught a whiff of smoke even as the horse
called Dickens squealed in alarm from the paddock
alongside the stable.

Sam cursed again as he began to run. He made it
across the open area and flattened himself against the
wooden wall of the barn to listen. The sound of fire
licking away at the dry hay was unmistakable. The
place would be an inferno in minutes. He pulled back
the slide on his automatic and stepped inside, just as
the overhead sprinkler system kicked in. An impossibly
loud siren shrilled, nearly deafening him.

Sam ignored both the water and the noise. He inched
forward slowly, hugging the wall as he approached the
nearest stall. He swiveled his head, trying to detect the

slightest movement. Nothing. Yet he sensed that he was not alone.

His stomach churned with acid as he peered into the first stall. Empty. He looked across the way and stopped moving altogether. A body lay crumpled in an untidy mound. The pitchfork embedded in its back seemed to sway.

Sam spun, looking for the person who had wielded the weapon. Still nothing stirred. He stepped forward slowly. A crunch sounded under his booted foot. Even in the deepening darkness, he saw the bent frame of broken glasses.

He shot a glance around him once again. There was no motion anywhere, but he could hear the flames overhead. The area darkened as the smoke spread outward. Dripping with water, he stepped inside the stall, keeping his back to the wall. He muttered an expletive as he hunkered down next to the body. He didn't need light to see the face. He knew who it belonged to. The pitchfork was buried so deep in the man's flesh, he knew the victim wouldn't survive. Still, he felt for a pulse.

Eyes fluttered open.

"Bill. Bill, can you hear me?"

The siren stopped as quickly as it had started. Light flooded the barn. Sam saw, rather than heard, his name on Bill's lips. Bill must have recognized his voice, because Sam knew the man was blind as a bat without his glasses.

"Hold on, buddy. I'll get you some help."

"Joe." Bill's hand made a feeble attempt to reach for him before it fell limply to the hard-packed earth.

Once again, Marly's gasp caught Sam unprepared. She stood in the opening, horror etched on her face. Before he could say a word, she whirled and ran. He

shoved his gun down his boot and stood, just as Carter
and Jake erupted through the main door.

"Cover the exits!" he yelled to them. "The perp may
still be inside!"

"What the—"

Carter ran forward and took one look, and his eyes
met Sam's.

"Marly went to call 911," Sam told him. At least
that was what he hoped she had done. "The person may
still be inside the barn. Seal off the exits."

"The fire…"

"I think the sprinklers have it under control."

Carter backed out and shouted to Jake and the other
two men. Sam turned back to Bill, but it was already
too late. The portly detective wouldn't have to worry
about his wife's diets ever again.

"Jesus, Bill. Why?"

"You know him?"

Sam's head jerked in surprise at Marly's question. "I
thought you went to call for help."

"I did. I used the phone in the tack room." Her eyes
returned to the body at his feet. "Oh, my God. Sam,
that's Officer Porterfield."

"Marly, get out of here. The guy who did this may
still be inside."

"Then what are you doing in here?"

Good question. He should be miles away and running
hard. Sam looked up at the sprinklers that continued to
rain down on them. "Drowning," he answered succinctly. "Come on, let's get outside." A sneeze punctuated his last word, and he cursed.

"You don't really think the murderer is still here, do
you?"

No, he didn't. Not anymore. But it had been a close

thing. The person had probably still been inside when he first entered.

"Not likely, but let's go. You shouldn't have turned on the lights with all this water running," he told her. Her hair lay plastered to her face, and her heavy robe was dragging on the ground.

"I didn't think. And what about you? You shouldn't even *be* in here. Your face is starting to swell again."

Damn it, he could feel that. Another sneeze tickled the back of his throat. His eyes were scratchy and beginning to water.

Marly headed toward the wall and the main light switch. Sam stopped her before she could touch it. "Let the fire department turn it off."

"Oh. What about Officer Porterfield? Is he—?"

"Yeah. He's dead."

Sam took a moment to study the inside of the barn, scratching absently at his arm. Bill hadn't been killed inside the stall. He'd been killed right here, near the door, probably pinned up against it by the thrust of the pitchfork. The scuff marks were still visible where he'd been dragged. That explained why his glasses were outside the stall.

"Sam?"

"Let's go."

Carter approached as they exited. His shirt hung unbuttoned against his well-muscled bare chest. His hair was mussed, but otherwise he was dressed much the way Sam was.

"I thought you said she went to call for help," Carter accused.

"I did," Marly told him. "I used the phone in the tack room."

"What about the guy inside?"

"Dead," Sam said succinctly.

"Sam implied the murderer might still be inside," Carter said suspiciously.

"I didn't know that then," Marly responded. Her eyes traveled to the roof. "It's still burning."

"Smoldering," Sam corrected, and sneezed again. He fumbled in his pocket for the antihistamine tablets. Carter hadn't seemed surprised that the victim was dead. He told himself it was a natural assumption to make, given the position of the pitchfork.

Lightning sizzled across the sky. Thunder rumbled in its wake. The breeze picked up, driving rain clouds before it. On the porch, Sam spotted five small forms huddled around Emma.

"You ought to go see to the kids," he told Marly.

She followed the direction of his nod and tipped her head to regard him. "Remember me? I'm the owner—you're the employee."

For just a second, he felt suitably chastised. He *had* forgotten. He was so used to being the one to give the orders.

"You ought to take something," Marly continued, more softly. "Your face is starting to swell again."

Sam wiggled the antihistamine tablets in front of her and swallowed two dry. "I'll wait here for the police."

"You won't have long to wait," Carter told him with a nod.

Sam followed his look to see a patrol car racing up the driveway, lights flashing, the siren on full. Fast service, even for a city. Unless the driver of the car had been nearby—maybe waiting for the call?

His stomach clenched so tight, Sam thought he might lose his dinner. The pills felt lodged in the back of his throat. It was possible that he could bluff his way through an initial police interview, but his avenues of escape were closing off fast.

A vivid burst of lightning forked the night sky. Thunder shattered the silence. Officer Duncan stepped from his car as the first drops of rain whipped toward them.

Chapter Seven

"What's going on here?" Duncan demanded.

Sam waited, but no one else spoke up. Resigned, he took two steps forward as thunder crashed overhead. "We've got a dead man in one of the stalls and a fire in the loft. You'd better call for backup." He punctuated his words with a sneeze.

Duncan's beady eyes narrowed. He looked as if he wanted to say something, but a sudden gust of smoke-filled wind seemed to make him decide against it. He ducked down into the car and lifted the radio.

"Come on," Marly said, taking Sam by the arm. "Let's get up on the porch. There's nothing we can do here now."

She was right. It was a sorry, wet group that trudged to the front porch and waited for the fire truck and the backup Duncan had radioed for.

"Why don't you go inside and change?" Sam suggested to Marly. She shook her head and shivered, watching as Duncan strode out of the brightly lit barn.

Sam felt a small hand reach for his. Jerome stood next to him, his chocolate eyes wide with anxiety. "It'll be okay, kid. You guys should go back inside before you get wet."

"Are you sick?" the boy asked.

Yeah. Of the entire situation. But Sam rubbed the child's head affectionately. "Just an allergy."

No one else moved except Emma. "Coffee," she stated, and disappeared in a swirl of housecoat.

"Okay. Who killed him?" Duncan asked, striding forward as though oblivious of the rain. No one spoke a word. Duncan's eyes immediately focused on Sam.

Belatedly Sam realized he hadn't taken time to put on his hat. He wondered if the scar on his head was covered by his wet hair. He didn't dare check. Fortunately, the rain and the sprinklers had plastered his hair to his face. He stood under Duncan's penetrating stare while lightning turned the porch to flashing moments of daylight.

"Who found the body?" Duncan asked.

"I did," Sam admitted.

"How did that come to happen? In the middle of the night, no less?"

For the first time, Sam realized Duncan wasn't in uniform. Like the other men on the porch, Duncan wore jeans. He also had on a casual plaid shirt, stretched tight across his broad shoulders. So he wasn't on duty. Sam couldn't see any bloodstains on his shirt, but he itched to ask the man how he'd come to be here so quickly. Prudence made him swallow the impulse.

"I spotted the fire from the window and went to investigate."

"I thought your room was in the front of the house, on the other side."

He and Marly spoke simultaneously.

"I was in the den."

"He was in my room."

Sam gave her a withering look. "Marly, don't—"

"Why was he in your room?"

Marly placed her hands on her hips and glared right back at Duncan. "Why do you think?"

"Marly."

She wouldn't look at Sam. Carter did, though. His expression was one of vitriolic hatred.

"I saw them come out of her room," Hector added.

Sam closed his eyes.

"They were whisperin' real loud, and Sam ran down the stairs," Zeke added helpfully.

Sam could see how it might have looked that way to the boys. The light spill had been coming from Marly's room, not his. It would be reasonable for the boys to assume they'd just come from her lit room, rather than his dark one.

A hook and ladder pulled into the narrow driveway, followed by not one, but three, county squad cars. Sam debated his options. "I'm going upstairs to put on a dry shirt," he announced.

"You'll stay right there," Duncan told him.

"You gonna make Marly and the others stand around soaking-wet, too?"

"This is stupid," Marly agreed. "The wind is tossing the rain on the porch. At least we can go inside."

She didn't wait for Duncan to respond. She opened the door and held it that way. "Come on, guys, inside." She didn't look at Sam.

While he'd never worked homicide, Sam knew the procedure. Separate the parties and take preliminary statements. They would focus on him, since he'd found the body. Should he stay with the alibi Marly had created, or go with the truth?

Why had she lied?

"OKAY, Mr. Moore, let's go over this one more time."

Sam waited patiently. He knew how the game was played, and at the moment, he was relieved the detective asking questions hadn't recognized him.

Maybe it wasn't so surprising, after all, given the way his face was swollen in reaction to the hay allergy. His damp hair effectively covered his scar, and what policeman would expect to see Officer Joe Walker on a horse farm in upper Montgomery County? Still, his luck couldn't hold much longer. With Porterfield identified, chances were good someone he knew would show up sooner or later—probably the captain himself. He had to get out of here.

What was Marly telling them? Had she heard Bill call him by name? What was she thinking?

Why had she lied?

"You were in Ms. Kramer's room, *talking,* when you spotted the fire from her window," the lanky detective continued.

"I spotted light in the loft of the barn," he corrected patiently. "I didn't realize it was a fire until I smelled the smoke, once I was outside."

"Ms. Kramer's a very attractive woman."

Sam sat silent in one of the red leather chairs in Marly's den, refusing to be provoked. The cop squinted at him, and Sam had to work to stay relaxed. The antihistamines were working. It wouldn't be long before his swollen, blotchy face returned to normal—or someone showed up who would recognize him anyway.

"You didn't see anyone? Hear anyone?"

"No, sir."

Never volunteer information. Stay as close to the truth as possible.

"You came here from Utah, you say?"

"Yes, sir."

"You sound like a Texas boy to me. Ever been there?"

On the money. Joseph Samuel Walker was born and raised there. How long before this guy made the connection?

"Yes, sir. Five years ago." He'd been home for his daddy's funeral.

"Okay, Sam," the detective said patiently, "you're the new guy around here. What's your take on these people?"

Sam shook his head. "I haven't had a chance to get to know anybody yet."

"Except Ms. Kramer."

He faced the challenge without blinking. It was an effort to keep a rein on his temper when this man mentioned Marly like that. He understood the maneuver, would have done the same thing in the officer's position. He kept his expression neutral. "That's right. Except Marly and the boys."

"Fast worker, huh? At least where Ms. Kramer's concerned."

Sam didn't respond.

The detective leaned forward, putting his face close enough so Sam could smell coffee on the man's breath. "You're telling me Ms. Kramer had no time or opportunity to go out to the barn and run a pitchfork through Officer Porterfield?"

Sam let his amusement show. "Do you really think she'd be strong enough?"

"You would."

Sam simply looked at him.

There was a sharp rap on the den door. A black officer arrived, and after a short conference he strode forward, a paper sack in his hand. He walked over to the desk and spilled the contents onto the blotter.

"Ever see this before?"

Sam tensed, staring at the wristwatch. He leaned forward, making a pretense of studying it without touching the item. "No, sir."

But he could make a damn good guess. He'd never actually *seen* Jerome's watch, but he'd have staked money that the object on the desk belonged to the kid. So what did that signify? Jerome sure as hell hadn't run a pitchfork through Porterfield.

"You're sure?"

Sam nodded. "I've never seen it before," he stated with complete assurance. The detective wasn't satisfied. He squinted at Sam, tipping his head as if puzzled by something. Sam felt his stomach clench tighter.

"You wear a watch, Mr. Moore?"

"No, sir."

"Never?"

"No, sir. Jewelry is dangerous when you work outside."

The cop replaced the watch in the evidence bag. Sam assumed it had already been dusted and photographed where it was found. After all, crews had been busy in the barn all night long. The rain had stopped some time ago, leaving daylight to filter across the sky.

"All right, Moore," he said, dropping the *Mr.* deliberately, Sam knew. "If you know anything, anything at all that might help us, now's the time to speak up."

"Nothing beyond what I've told everyone for the past two hours."

The two men leaned back and exchanged glances. The lanky one rubbed at his eyes and frowned. "Okay. That's all for now. We're going to ask that you keep yourself available for questioning until we get to the bottom of this.''

Sam stood, tired to the core, every muscle in his body screaming in protest. ''Yes, sir.'' He felt their eyes as he left the room.

The house was surprisingly silent, considering all the people who seemed to be ranging in and out. Sam wandered out to the kitchen. Emma looked up from the stove, gave him one of her precious smiles and reached for a coffee mug. Without a word, she poured him a cup and handed it to him.

''Emma, I may have to marry you,'' he told her.

Her smile lit her plump face, and she gestured toward a chair at the table. Sam sank down, too tired to go anywhere else. ''Have you seen Marly?''

The smile disappeared under a wreath of concern. Emma shook her head, her chins quivering, and turned back to the stove, breaking eggs into a pan. Sam sighed as he sipped at the hot brew, letting the caffeine soak into his bloodstream. Maybe it would help keep him awake. He needed a clear head and some time to think. Right now, he didn't have either one. The only thought that hung unclouded was the knowledge that he needed to leave. Today. The sooner the better. Once they named him, they wouldn't look any farther—except at Marly, who had alibied him.

Emma slid a plate of bacon and eggs in front of him. Sam looked up and gave her a weak smile. ''Thanks, Emma, but I don't think I can do it.''

''You need to eat.''

It was the longest sentence he had ever heard her speak. He was touched by her concern. Unable to hurt her feelings, Sam lifted his fork. Emma smiled in satisfaction and went to refill his coffee cup. By the time he'd finished the food, Sam was surprised at how much better he felt. He stood and carried his dishes to the sink, rinsing off his plate under her watchful eyes.

"You're a treasure, Emma." He placed a gentle kiss on her forehead. "Take care of Marly for me."

"Leaving?"

"Not because I want to." He realized that was the truth. He didn't want to go, particularly now, when Marly would really need him. But he'd do her no good in jail.

Emma's eyes were sharp and crystal blue as she studied him. "You'll be back," she stated.

He patted her shoulder. "I hope so."

As he passed, he saw that the den was empty now. Sam stopped and considered. There was only one person in a position to help him at this point. He entered the room, shut the door and lifted the receiver.

George Brent's telephone rang unanswered. Surprised, he stared at the instrument. Even if George was working on a big case, his wife should be home at this hour. Unless they were out of town.

Sam hung up and dialed a different number.

"Yeah?" the voice snarled in greeting after the third ring.

"We're really going to have to do something about your telephone habits, Lee. If I was a beautiful woman, I'd hang up and never call again."

"God damn it, Joe, if you were a beautiful woman, you'd have more sense than to call me at weird hours. Where the hell are you, anyhow?"

"It doesn't matter, I won't be here two minutes from now. Listen up, I've got problems."

"Tell me something I don't know."

Sam could almost see his partner shoving his hands

through his dark hair. "Porterfield was murdered last night."

There was a beat of silence. "You're kidding me, right?"

"I'm pretty sure he was the one on the take. If we can prove that, it will go a long way to proving my innocence. I'm betting he's the one who killed Rayback and framed me."

Lee hesitated for several more seconds. "Then who killed him?"

Sam closed his eyes in frustration, then opened them to stare out the window. The yellow streamer cordoning off the barn fluttered as a breeze batted at it. "That could get complicated, and it may have nothing to do with my situation—except that I was Joey-on-the-spot again."

Lee cut loose a string of profanity. "I don't effing believe this. You were there? When Porterfield got iced? Don't you know any better?"

"Apparently not. You're on the inside, partner. I'm working blind here."

"God. I could wring your neck myself."

"You're going to have to stand in line."

Lee sighed. "No doubt. What do you need?"

"See what you can dig up on a Montgomery County cop by the name of Johnny Duncan. Also, check a man by the name of Carter Delancy and one known as Jake Smith. They both work on a horse farm in upper Montgomery County."

Again there was silence on the other end. Finally he heard Lee release a hard breath of air on yet another expletive. "You want to fill in some of the blanks for me, Joe?"

"Later. I could be interrupted at any moment. I'll call you around six tonight. Will you be home?"

"Make it after eight. This is going to take time. I may have to explain what I'm doing to the captain."

Sam frowned. "Where is George, anyhow? I just tried to call him."

"Well, thank God for that. He asked me if I'd heard from you."

Sam wasn't sure how to respond to that, but Lee continued without waiting.

"I told him no, but I don't think he believed me. He said if you called to tell you to check in."

"He actually said that?"

"I think we could use his help, Joe."

"Like I said, I tried, but there wasn't any answer."

"Maybe he's on his way to the scene where Porterfield got taken out."

"What about Cassandra?"

"Beats me. No one's seen her in weeks. She's probably visiting with her dad."

Sam nodded to himself. He knew her father had cancer. "Yeah. Thanks, partner. I owe you big-time."

"Don't worry, I'll collect."

Sam hung up. It was past time to get out of here. He felt marginally better knowing he had two good cops in his corner, but the last thing he wanted was to be trapped here and made the prime suspect in Bill's death, as well. He headed for the stairs.

Marly's bedroom door was closed when he reached the landing. He stared at the silent wood, debating. It had been hours since he'd seen her. He knew she'd been exhausted. She'd probably gone inside to lie down and rest. He'd pack first, then he'd wake her. He never questioned that he would tell her he was leaving.

He turned to his own room and opened the door. Marly was asleep on his bed.

"Damn."

She didn't stir. She lay on her side, facing him, her creamy skin devoid of makeup. She didn't need artifice, he decided. She had a natural beauty that stirred a man's blood. Her soft peach lips drew his gaze, as always.

Sam sighed and turned away, heading for the dresser. As he began shoving his meager belongings into his duffel bag, he studied her reflection in the mirror. She wore a pink cotton shirt and a clean pair of denims, both of which hugged every delectable curve of her body. Her hair, long and loose, spilled over one shoulder. He would carry that image away with him, as well.

Her eyes blinked open. "Sam?"

He turned, zipping the bag.

"You're leaving?"

It was hard—harder than it should have been. "Yes."

She sat up, the imprint of his pillow on her left cheek. She looked flushed and tousled, and so fragile that it hurt.

"Why?"

"Marly—"

"What do they want you for?"

Her question didn't surprise him. He ran a rough hand over his scratchy jaw. "Murder."

Her mouth opened. She closed it as she regarded him steadily, and then her head moved slowly from side to side. "You didn't do it."

That bare statement plundered his ulcer, setting fire to his stomach. "How can you say that? What if I did?"

"Then it was self-defense."

"Marly—"

Her gaze was unswerving. "I know you, Sam. I've watched you. You wouldn't murder anyone."

Her absolute belief stunned him as nothing else could have. She was too honest and trusting for her own good. "Jesus! You don't know anything. You barely know me. For all you know, I killed Porterfield."

Marly didn't flinch. Her eyes held steady on him. "Did you?"

Sam uttered an expletive. "I don't believe this. What do you think?"

Marly sat up and swung her legs off the bed. Anger to match his own spit from her eyes. "I think that since you've shown up at my farm I'm in more trouble than I've ever been in my whole life."

"Look, I'm sorry about that, but—"

"Oh, sorry, are you? Well, you can stick that in your duffel bag too, cowboy. I went to bat for you down there."

"I never asked—"

"No, you didn't. But my life's going down the tubes here, Sam, and I damn well don't deserve your anger. You knew Porterfield. I heard you when you found him. You were shocked." Her voice softened. "I'm sorry about your friend. Is your name really Joe?"

He swore again, viciously.

"Talk to me. Let me help you. We can help each other." She stood and walked toward him.

"You can't help me, and all I can do is cause you more trouble. You shouldn't have lied to the cops. I shouldn't have let you. They're going to be all over you when they find out I'm gone."

"Why did you come here?"

The question stopped him when he would have pushed past her. "I needed a place to hide."

"No. It was more than that. Chris recognized you, didn't he? I saw it when Duncan pulled up after the grass fire."

He tensed, unwittingly. "Marly, you're too observant for your own good. Is that why you lied? To protect me? They're going to be wild when they find out."

"How will they find out, unless you tell them?"

"Don't you understand? The police will descend on this place like charging elephants after I leave. You don't want to know anything more than what they tell you."

She shook her head, her long hair swinging gently. "Let me help you."

"You can't."

"Don't be so sure. Why did you come here?" Her demand was impatient this time.

Sam knew he should walk out the door without another word. George was probably pulling up the long driveway while he stood here. But one look at her stubborn face and he knew he couldn't walk away without giving her some explanation. "I needed Chris."

That rocked her. "Why?"

"He's the only witness to the murder."

"My God, Sam, he's just a boy."

"In the city, boys grow up real fast."

She nodded weary agreement. "Is he going to help you?"

"He's a scared kid, Marly."

"Is that why he ran away?"

Sam shrugged, hating the question, because it was one he kept asking himself. "Probably. Either that or he saw something else that night that scared him."

"The person with the goat?"

"Maybe. I just don't know."

The frown faded beneath the resolute expression that set her lips in a decisive line. "Come on. We'll put your duffel bag in the truck, so you can leave from the hospital once you talk to Chris."

He shook his head. "I'm going out the back way, on foot. They'll be watching me—"

"They'll be watching *us* as we run Chris's belongings into town before he's discharged," she said, interrupting him. "He isn't coming back, you know. As soon as they release him, he's going to stay with an aunt in Ohio."

"Ohio!"

"Do you want to talk to him or not, Sam?"

"Marly, I can't let you risk—"

"Life's a risk. Besides, if I'm not here, maybe the authorities will wait a little longer before they close me down."

Her pained expression tore at him. He hadn't thought about it, but she was right. Between Chris getting injured and Porterfield being murdered, the authorities would have little recourse but to pull the kids from her program.

"Marly, I'm sorry. I should never have involved you or—"

"Come on. We won't have to sneak. You walk out to the truck, and I'll let someone in authority know where we're going. Emma will keep an eye on the boys until I get back."

"Marly, it isn't even seven o'clock in the morning. I don't think anyone is going to buy our going to the hospital to visit Chris at this hour."

"You'd be amazed. I can be very persuasive."

She had that right. He must be completely exhausted. That was the only reason he could think of to be contemplating going with her—if George didn't arrive and stop him.

"They're releasing Chris at ten. We have to get there early if we want to see him."

"Marly—"

"Put your hat on. Your scar is showing."

He'd have to stop underestimating this woman. Her ex-husband must have been a total jerk to let her escape.

Fifteen minutes later, they were in her truck, tooling down the twisty two-lane road. Sam released a sigh as he shifted gears.

"What sort of work do you really do, Sam?"

He gave her an amused grin. "You don't believe I'm a ranch hand?"

"Not with your allergy."

"Maybe that's why I came east. Maybe the allergy was getting so bad I thought I could take a break, find a decent allergist and go back when I had it under control."

"Are you telling me that's the truth?"

He found her eyes watching him steadily and discovered he couldn't lie to her anymore. "No."

"Didn't think so."

Her complacent reaction disturbed him. "Why not?"

"Your hands lack the right calluses, and you could barely walk after riding a horse for half an hour. That's not a man used to ranching, Sam."

"Yeah, well, it's been a while."

"Uh-huh. So what do you really do?"

"When I'm not being framed for murder, I'm a cop."

Her silence deafened him. He shot her a glance. The frightening mix of expressions on her face provoked his ulcer. Was she horrified? Angry? Relieved? Sam pulled off to the side of the road. Marly didn't even seem to notice. "What's wrong?"

She wouldn't look at him. He couldn't tell what she was thinking, but he could tell something was very wrong.

"Marly, what is it?" He reached for her hand and found it icy-cold to the touch. "Look, I know you probably don't have any reason to love cops, but we're not all like Duncan, you know."

She did look at him then. Her eyes were dark, fathomless pools. "Oh, I know, Sam. I was married to one. Some of you are worse."

"So that's it." He released her fingers, pulled off his hat and ran his fingers through his hair, cursing under his breath. "Great. Just great."

"I don't think so."

The edge to her words brought his eyes back to her face. "What's that supposed to mean? Look, I'm not going to apologize for what I do. I'm a cop. I'm proud to be a cop. It's a job I'm good at, and—"

"You don't have to sell your work to me. I know all about the brotherhood of policemen."

This time there was something missing from her tone. It didn't contain the anger or frustration he expected. It was almost devoid of emotion. Sort of the way she had spoken to Duncan that first day. A prickle of anxiety worked its way up his spine.

"You want to tell me what's going on here, Marly?"

"You don't get it, do you, Sam?"

"Obviously not. What am I supposed to be getting?"

"Tell me about the murder."

"Marly—"

"Just humor me, okay?"

He was spooked. She had such an odd expression on

her face. All his alarm bells were going off, but for the life of him, Sam couldn't figure out why.

Haltingly, he told her about Rayback. He told her how they had set things up to catch Rayback with the evidence and how the money had gone missing. She never said a word, and her eyes didn't waver from his face.

It was hard, but he told her about the other officers who were suspects, about Bill and Lee and how later—after the murder—some of the evidence had been found in Sam's own apartment.

Then he told her about that night. About his gun being switched. "Ballistics proved my gun was the one that killed Rayback. I was holding it when they found me. My prints were the only ones on it. In my favor was the fact it was the only weapon at the scene and it was obvious I had been shot, too." He touched the scar on his head.

"Wouldn't that prove you didn't do it?"

"I wish. They had several theories, but their favorite was that I hadn't acted alone. Thank God Lee had a cast-iron alibi for the time period."

Marly was quiet for a moment. "How did Chris come to be at the scene?"

"That's one of the questions I plan to ask him."

He told her about Chris and the shadowy figure who'd done the shooting. He told her of his own escape from the hospital when he'd realized where the questions were heading and that the investigation wasn't focusing on anyone else. Then he told her how his captain had identified Chris as the possible witness. How Sam's efforts to track the boy had led directly to her place.

Marly sat quietly, her hands folded almost primly in

her lap. A cardinal flew across the road, its noisy cry startling him.

He wished he hadn't eaten breakfast. The coffee burned in the back of his throat. His stomach churned in an attempt to deal with the worst case of nerves he had suffered from in a long time. Why didn't she say something? Why did she look so odd?

"The thing I don't understand," Sam said pensively, "is why Porterfield sent Chris to your horse farm. He must have known Chris would recognize him as the murderer."

Marly's face clearly showed her shock. "You think Officer Porterfield was the one who shot you and killed—?"

"Who else? The captain said it had to be one of the four of us. According to Bill himself, we were the only ones with the opportunity inside the evidence room. Now Bill's been murdered, and I'm conveniently at hand—again."

Marly stared at him.

"Don't worry," he snarled, gripping the steering wheel. "You don't have to look so scared. You aren't the next victim."

"I never thought that, Sam. Not for a minute. I know you didn't kill anyone."

"Will you stop saying that? You can't possibly know that. You don't know anything about me." He stared at the road, fighting panic. "I couldn't be sitting in a more indefensible position."

"You don't know who Rayback was, do you, Sam?" she asked finally.

"Kind of an odd question, isn't it?"

"No, not really. They didn't release the information." He stared at her, wondering anew at her strange expression. "How would you know information about a murder that wasn't released?" Aggravation sharpened his voice. "What's going on here, Marly? What sort of game are you playing?" Fear gnawed at him. There was an undercurrent here that he didn't understand.

Her eyes clouded in sorrow. "It's no game, Sam. I know all about the murder. As his next of kin, they had to tell me."

He stared at her. "What did you say?" The words sounded raw. That was just how he felt.

"The police asked me to keep the information to myself until they were ready to release the whole story. Until they caught you."

He wasn't sure what he'd expected, but it sure as hell wasn't her calm statement. His weary mind focused on one fact. "You're Rayback's next of kin?"

Her words echoed in his head. She was related to Rayback? How could she be related to a slimy piece of work like that?

She nodded.

Sam was suspicious of coincidence. Any good cop was. Yet here he was, facing an entire string of them. He had arrived at Marly's place with no clue that she was related to the victim—or that Porterfield was the one who had sent Chris to her horse farm. His stomach churned as he considered the ramifications.

"You still don't get it, do you?" she asked.

"Oh, I get it okay. They're going to fry me for murder. What was he, your brother, uncle, cousin—what?"

"Worse, Sam. He was my husband."

Chapter Eight

"My God, and you told the cops I was sleeping with you."

Marly was stunned. Sam's response—so unlike her ex-husband's—made clear his first thoughts were concern for her. When would he make the terrible connection that was suddenly all too clear to her?

"What does what I told the police have to do with anything?" she demanded. "I was trying to help you."

Sam or Joe, or whatever his name really was, put the car back in gear. "I'd say you helped, all right. We'll be lucky if this case even gets to trial."

Marly reached out and touched his jacketed arm, aware once again of the strength of this man. "I don't understand. You should be glad I told them we were together. At least I've given you an alibi for last night's killing."

"And yourself a motive for being an accessory to murder," he said tersely.

Stunned, she stared at his stern profile. "How do you figure that?"

"If you and I were lovers, as the police believe, I'd have an even better reason for helping you get rid of your ex."

Marly withdrew her hand. "That's crazy. I was already rid of him."

"Did you get a good settlement?"

"What kind of question is that?"

Apprehension sharpened her tone, because the answer was a resounding no. It was one of the reasons she was in a financial bind this year. She'd been so anxious to get rid of Matt after discovering his countless infidelities, she hadn't listened to her lawyer's advice. She'd only wanted her husband to disappear from her life. Him and his chronic lying, cheating ways. Even now, she didn't regret that decision.

"From your silence, I'll take that as a no. How long have you been divorced?"

"Officially? Seven months."

"Did he have a will?"

She stared at him. "Sam, what are you getting at?" But she was very much afraid she knew the answer.

"These questions are the same ones the cops will use to build a case against us."

"Us?"

"As in you and me, kid. As in collusion to collect his insurance and anything he might have left you in a will."

Marly gasped. "That's crazy!"

"No will?"

Nerves hammered at her. "Matt did have a will," she admitted reluctantly. "We had them drawn up shortly after we were married."

Sam groaned. "Making each other beneficiaries, right?"

Her heart thumped painfully. "He could have changed his."

"Like you did?"

Of course she hadn't. She hadn't even thought about the blasted wills. Odds were Matt hadn't, either.

"I'll take that as another no."

"Sam, he wasn't rich. No one would believe that I—that you and I..."

Of course they would. Sam was good-looking, in a virile way that would attract any normal woman. Last night, the two of them had nearly ended up on his bed. She hadn't exactly been pushing him away. Sam was right. She'd given the officers a reason to believe they were sleeping together. "No! It's completely crazy. I didn't even know you before my divorce."

"Tell it to the investigators."

His pithy tone silenced her. Had she really set herself up as a murder suspect? Sam painted a grim picture.

"Damn!"

His sudden curse drew her eyes to his lean thighs and the long leg that was pumping the brake pedal. "What's the matter? What's wrong with the brakes?"

Sam didn't respond. His knuckles whitened on the steering wheel. He downshifted, eyes focused ahead. Her eyes flicked to the dashboard. There was no warning light showing, but they weren't slowing down. Her breath caught in her throat. "What's wrong?"

"No brakes."

"None at all?"

"No, damn it."

"The brake light isn't on."

"I know that," he almost snarled.

Marly clamped her lips together. She couldn't afford to distract him. This narrow stretch of road was posted at fifty miles an hour. Sam was doing close to sixty, and they were approaching a blind curve. Trees lined the road on both sides.

Sam tried the emergency brake, without success. "Hang tight, and pray no one is coming at us," he said.

They crossed the double yellow line as they reached the curve. It wasn't enough. Sam fought the wheel, trying to hold the car on the road. For just a moment, Marly thought he'd make it, but the bend was too sharp, they were moving too fast. The back end slewed. The truck spun as it clipped a tree.

Her eyes clamped shut, and she bit down on her lip to stifle a scream. The truck veered out of control. The bouncing, jolting roller-coaster ride lasted forever. She was flung against the seat belt, the side window, and Sam. Her arm struck something with a jarring thud as the vehicle began to topple down the incline, into the field below. Glass and metal gave way with brittle sounds as the truck tumbled and slid along its side.

It shuddered to a sliding, grinding halt, resting on the driver's side. The abrupt silence was deafening. Marly lifted her head and opened her eyes. The windshield was a shattered vision of starred cracks and missing pieces. All she could see was the top of the raised hood, which had sprung open.

The seat belt pinned her awkwardly, painfully in place. She tasted blood and realized she must have bitten her lip. Glass shards littered the inside of the car. She twisted to look at Sam. His eyes were closed. Several small cuts laced his hands and his face. Wedged against his door, his head rested on the side window, which, miraculously, remained intact. He didn't move.

"Sam?"

He didn't respond.

Fear clenched her heart. She reached out to shake his shoulder. "Sam!"

His eyes fluttered open, and he groaned. Only then

did she release the air trapped in her frightened lungs. "Sam, are you okay?"

He blinked, groggily surveying the scene. "Hell of a ride," he muttered.

It was an effort not to throw up. She swallowed back the bile and tried to sound calm. "Personally, I prefer my rides in amusement parks." She was proud of the control in her voice, even as she inwardly thanked God that Sam hadn't died. "Are you okay?" she asked again.

"I think so. I'm just trying to absorb the fact that we're still alive and not wrapped around some tree. My guardian angel must have called in a few favors." He flexed his muscles one by one, as though testing for injuries. "Nothing seems to be broken. How about you?"

Marly experimented. Apart from a little stiffness, she felt okay. Nothing screamed in protest when she moved. She probed her puffy lip and decided it was the worst of her injuries. "Everything seems to be in working order."

"Good. Let's see if we can get out of here."

Marly raised her head toward her door. It was shut snugly, slightly askew in its metal frame. They wouldn't be opening that in any hurry. "How?"

"With extreme care." He glanced from the window on her side of the cab to the shattered windshield. "Not much room in here to maneuver." He released his seat belt with a sharp click. "I'm going to climb over the back. That rear window is designed to be kicked out."

"It is?"

"Trust me."

"What are my other options?"

Sam gave her a lopsided grin. "Stay in your belt until I'm over the seat. I'll try not to kick you in the face."

"I'd appreciate that."

Holding her shoulder belt, she pulled herself upward against gravity to give him as much room as possible. His boot nearly did catch her in the head as he went over the seat into the narrow back bench.

"Stay put until I clear this Plexiglas."

"I don't think I'm going anywhere for the moment," she responded tartly. Sam didn't bother to answer. He pressed his back against the driver's seat and used his feet on the rear window. In minutes, he had popped the Plexiglas out of the way.

"Now let's get out of here."

Without Sam's help, there was no way she would have made it out of the cab. She felt weak and shaky as he helped her through the small opening into the twisted bed of the truck. He lifted her down onto the grass, and for a long time she just stood in the field and stared at the remains of the vehicle.

Sam brushed at the bits of glass that clung to his shirt as he began examining the undercarriage of the car. He moved on to the exposed engine, not touching a thing. Eventually he turned back to her.

"You sure you're okay?"

Marly brushed a strand of hair out of her mouth. "Peachy. Why were you looking at the bottom of the truck like that? And don't you dare tell me the brake line was cut."

He cocked his head to look at her. "Why not?"

"Because it's trite, damn it. I've seen it done on every cop show on television. No one does that in real life. No one except a mechanic even knows what a brake line looks like. Besides, there's no reason for anyone to have tampered with my brakes."

A suspicion of a smile edged the corners of his

mouth. "Come on. We need to flag someone down and get you to the hospital."

"I didn't hit my head, Sam. You don't have to humor me."

He did grin then. "Okay, but I hit mine, and it hurts like hell. Can we humor *me* instead?"

"Oh. I didn't know. Let me see." Contrite and embarrassed, she stared at him, really looking for the first time since the accident.

"I'm fine," he said. "We're both lucky."

As he turned back to regard the truck, she saw the left side of his face. A bruise was forming near his temple, not far from his scar.

"You *are* hurt."

"I told you that."

She stuck out her tongue in a childish gesture of relief.

"Cute." He grinned at her.

She stared at the bruise on his head. "Somehow, I think of you as invincible. The bruise surprises me."

"Thanks. I think."

All humor left his expression as they stood there. He studied her with an intensity that touched her soul. For just a moment, she felt connected to this man. Then he blinked, and the moment dissolved.

"Are you going to let me look at your head?"

He touched his hand to the site and probed tenderly. "It's just bruised, Doc. Besides, I like seeing two of you."

"Sam, don't."

His nod at the rebuke was so slight she almost missed it. "I must have smacked into the side window when we rolled."

"I still can't believe we rolled down the embankment."

"Well, we sure didn't float down on a cloud of fairy dust." They both regarded the scene. "I'm just damn glad this was such a big, sturdy old truck and we were wearing seat belts."

"Me too."

He pulled out a white handkerchief and wrapped it around a cut on his hand that was bleeding.

"Want me to take a look at that?" she offered.

"Nope. Superficial. There's no glass in it."

"It should be cleaned."

"See any first-aid stuff lying around?"

"There's some in the truck."

Sam nodded toward the crumpled metal. "Want to climb back in and find it?"

She shook her head.

"Me either. Think you can make it to the road?"

She eyed the uphill grade. It wasn't a mountain, nor even a steep hill, but there wasn't a chance. She suddenly felt shaky and extremely brittle.

"Of course I can," she lied.

Sam grinned, one of his cocky I-like-you grins that warmed her heart and made her think she could do just about anything with this man at her side.

That was a scary thought. Much too close to emotions she wasn't ready to explore. For the first time, she realized that not only had he helped her out of the truck, and gotten himself out, as well, he was still holding his much-battered Stetson in his other hand. She seized on that fact as they started walking.

"Do you sleep with that hat on?"

Sam laughed, a deep, throaty laugh that warmed the cold places inside her. He tapped her nose, still chuckling. "Only if I can't find a better companion. We'll talk about it tonight. Come on."

A thrill of excitement coursed through her. Tonight. That sounded like he planned to stay. Like he planned to share the night with her.

She all but snuggled against the strength of the arm he slid about her shoulders, because her legs had turned to overcooked noodles. Shock, she decided. Now that everything was over, her body was reacting with a giant case of nerves. Getting to the road seemed a colossal task.

Sam made it easy. She liked the feel of his arm around her far more than she should have. "Was the brake line cut?" she asked finally to keep thoughts of him at bay.

"Maybe not, but brakes don't quit all of a sudden like that due to any natural condition I know of. There should have been some warning that something was wrong."

"I don't believe it." But she did. Someone had tampered with her truck. Sam didn't reply, and together they staggered onto the shoulder of the road.

"Why would someone do that?" she asked.

"Why would someone want to hang a baby goat in your barn?"

She forgot her rubbery legs and her aching muscles. A hot surge of pure anger swept through her. She pulled free, planted her feet and glared at Sam. "The goat is one thing, but we could have been killed in that accident."

"This just occurred to you?"

"No. Yes. I don't know. I'm not thinking clearly yet. But I want him arrested," she announced. "I want the person who did this found and hanged. Then I want to spit on his grave."

Sam tipped his head, looking both amused and appreciative at the same time. "Bloodthirsty wench, aren't you?"

"Yes."

"I'll have to remember that."

"Do that. And after we find out who did this and he's dead and buried, I'm going to relocate. Someplace where the suburbs aren't encroaching."

"Utah's nice," Sam said mildly.

"Okay. I'll look there. Will you come with me?" The words were out before she could stop them. "Sorry. I forgot." She turned and started walking.

"Marly—"

"Don't, Sam. We both know this attraction for what it is."

"We do, huh? What is it, exactly?"

"A chemical attraction," she said in exasperation. "You're a cop and I'm a misplaced cowgirl."

He scratched his jaw, looking perplexed and amused at the same time. "What the hell do you mean, a chemical attraction? You like my after-shave?"

"You know what I mean, you're just fishing."

Sam tipped back his hat, his dark eyes regarding her. "Am I catching anything?"

She forced a smile. "You can tease all you like. I still think you're sexy as hell."

He paused, a comical expression of astonishment on his face. "You sure pick your moments, lady."

"Timing is everything." She shrugged, and quickly wished she hadn't. Between the well and the car wreck, her muscles were annoyed.

They walked several more feet in silence. She wondered what Sam was thinking, and she was mildly surprised that no cars had passed them yet. "Who tampered with my brakes, Sam?"

"Someone who knew what he was doing."

"Why do you say that?"

"Like you said before, messing with brake lines isn't something a novice can do. You've got more than one line, and a gauge to tell you when your fluid level drops below a certain point."

"The warning light for the brakes didn't come on," she pointed out.

"Exactly, yet none of the brake system worked after we stopped to talk."

Marly thought about that for a few minutes. "Was it the same person who killed Porterfield?"

"I think that's a logical assumption."

She concentrated on placing one foot in front of the other. "Thinking is a little beyond me at the moment. I'm just responding and reacting. Shock, you know. I think I've had one too many. Chris runs away, I find myself suspended over a bottomless well, Porterfield gets murdered, and someone screws up my brakes. This is much worse than a bad hair day."

Sam chuckled and gave her shoulder an avuncular pat. "What do you know about Carter and Jake?"

That brought her to a complete standstill as his meaning struck her. "You think one of them—?"

He rested a hand on her shoulder. "I'm just exploring possibilities."

"Yeah, well, I don't like those possibilities. Carter's been with me a long time. I've relied heavily on him since my marriage fell apart."

"He wants you."

"I know."

She started walking again more briskly. Sam lengthened his stride to keep pace beside her.

"It's become a problem recently," she admitted. "We had a long talk on the way back from the hospital. It wasn't pleasant. I know Carter was angry, but he wouldn't have fooled with my brake lines."

"He'd know how."

Surprised, she could only nod. Carter did a lot of tinkering on the older, red pickup truck. She wasn't sure how Sam knew this, but maybe Carter had mentioned it.

"What about Jake?" Sam persisted.

"I doubt if he even knows how to open the hood. He's a horseman." At Sam's frown, she shrugged, and again wished she hadn't, as several muscles complained. "Jake's not so bad. Surly, and a bit cocky, but he's a good worker and he's great with horses. He used to be a jockey, a long time ago."

They walked a bit farther before Sam broached a new subject. "How did you come to be privy to inside police information?"

She tilted her head in surprise. "I'm not. I was only asked not to say anything about the murder."

"Why? It was on every television station in the metropolitan area."

"The murder was, but not his real identity."

"What are you talking about?" It was Sam's turn to come to a standstill at the side of the road.

Taking in his expression, she realized they hadn't been communicating very well. "I thought you knew," she said softly.

"Apparently I don't know squat." He pinned her with his dark eyes. "You're saying Rayback had another identity?"

"His name wasn't Rayback. His name was Kramer, Matthew Kramer."

Sam's face hardened to granite. "I figured Kramer was your maiden name—that you took it back after the divorce."

"No. You didn't kill Alan Rayback."

"I didn't kill anyone!"

Flustered, she stared at him. Had she once thought his eyes were safe? They were obsidian and ice right now. "Don't you remember? I told you my husband—ex-husband—was a cop. He was working undercover."

"A cop?" To say Sam was stunned would have been a granddaddy of an understatement. This time, her hand went out to steady him, noting the tenseness of the muscles bunched beneath the material of his jacket. Sam didn't even seem to notice her hand. "You never said he was a cop."

"You really didn't know." The fact was somehow frightening.

He shook his head, never taking his dark eyes from her, but she didn't think he was actually seeing her.

"Matt was on loan to the D.C. force. He's actually a Montgomery County cop. Was a cop," she amended. It was hard to think of him as dead. And the man standing next to her, the man she was so impossibly attracted to, was the man accused of killing him. How absurd.

"Did he work for internal affairs?"

"I don't think so. While we were married, he mostly worked vice."

Sam stood for several long minutes before he started walking again. She could almost hear him trying to fit things together. "Did Rayba—your husband—know Porterfield?"

"I doubt it. Matt wasn't around much last summer.

We only shared joint occupancy because his lawyer told him not to move out, but he was seldom home. Matt didn't approve of my youth program."

"But Porterfield could have seen him?"

"I guess. It's possible, I suppose."

"Your husband was rather distinctive, with that shock of white hair."

"Ex-husband." She tried to curb her bitterness. "Yes, he was distinctive, all right. He looked like a young John Forsythe. Women found him devastating."

He tipped his head in her direction. "Yourself included, I presume?"

"Once. It didn't take me long to discover how hard it was to compete with his most adoring fan. His mirror."

Sam's lips quirked, and she turned away in embarrassment. "I didn't mean to say that."

"Why not? It was the impression I got, too. A real lady-killer."

"Yeah. That was Matt, all right. But he was a good cop, Sam." She felt compelled to add that last, because whatever else Matt might have been, he'd been proud of the work he did.

Sam reached for her hand. His touch was warm and reassuring. "I assume, since you worked together, Bill at least knew what your husband did for a living?"

"Yes. Of course."

"So when he saw Rayback up close, chances are he would have recognized Rayback as your husband."

"If he ever saw Matt, I'm sure he would have." It was obvious where Sam was headed. "You think Officer Porterfield killed Matt?"

"Yeah. Bill must have removed the evidence from the evidence room before he learned Rayback's real identity. He would have panicked when he realized it was a trap. He came into the bar, handed us the story about internal affairs, looked for an opportunity to frame one of us, and I conveniently gave him an immediate opening. The rest, as they say, is history."

"But if that's the case, who killed Porterfield?"

At the sound of a car approaching from behind them, Sam pulled her farther off the side of the road and stepped forward to flag it down. The driver was coming on slowly, and he spotted them at once. He coasted to a stop and stepped partially out of his sedan.

"You two belong to that pickup truck back there?"

"Yes, sir. The brakes went," Sam explained.

"Are you hurt?"

"Bruised and battered. Nothing serious."

"You're lucky. I was just on my way to find a telephone. Hop in and I'll give you a lift to the hospital."

"Thanks."

Tuning out the conversation, Marly let Sam handle the introductions and explanations. She couldn't stop the chaotic flow of her thoughts. Sam's situation was overwhelming. It was so hard to believe he was connected, even peripherally, to her ex-husband's death. She didn't want to think about it. She particularly didn't want to think about how it might tie into her own problems, but Sam had firmly planted the seeds of doubt about her staff. She just couldn't see how the two were related.

The threatening phone calls had started before Sam showed up. Yet they had emanated from the bunkhouse, and Jake was the one who'd answered the phone. Somehow, she didn't want Jake to be guilty of terrorizing her, but who did that leave? Keefer? Lou?

Carter was the obvious suspect. He had been furious

when he found out she told Porterfield about the calls
and the incidents that had been plaguing her. His anger
had seemed oddly misplaced, even at the time. Had he
been furious because he was behind those incidents?
Because he was afraid the police would investigate?

Why *had* Porterfield gone to her barn last night? He'd
told her his family was leaving on vacation. Could she
really believe Carter or Jake capable of murder, or was
all this related to Sam and, ultimately, to her ex-
husband?

"Here you go, folks."

She looked up to see the hospital emergency room in
front of them. "Come on. Let's get you examined,"
Sam said.

"No. I—"

"Thanks for coming to our rescue," Sam said to the
driver.

"You sure you don't want me to wait and give you
a lift someplace?"

"No, thanks. Her brother will come as soon as we
call. Thanks again. Appreciate it."

Sam slipped from the car and helped her from the
seat. Her muscles protested every movement, shocking
her with their stiffness.

"I don't have a brother," she said quietly as they
watched their rescuer drive off.

"Me either, but wait till you meet my sister." His
grin cheered her. "You talked to her already."

"I did?"

"Mrs. Norton. My reference?"

"That was your sister? No wonder she gave you such
an outstanding recommendation."

"Yeah. She thought she was helping me with a police
cover when I called her."

"She doesn't know you're in trouble?"

"Nope. And when she finds out the truth and gets her hands on me, she'll wring my neck. Come on, we'll get you checked out."

Marly protested. "You can't afford to waste that kind of time, can you, Sam?"

"I didn't say I was gonna let them check me."

"That's what I thought. I feel fine." It was only a tiny white lie. "Let's go see Chris instead."

"Marly, I think you should let a doctor look at you. We were jounced around pretty good when that truck rolled."

"And that cut on your hand should be washed out, and the bruise on your head looked at, as well." He frowned, and she pushed home the point. "I guess you won't scare Chris to death looking like that. Let's go talk to him."

"You're a stubborn woman, you know that?"

"Thank you." The automatic doors swung inward, and Marly strode inside, ignoring the fear in her mind and the twinges her muscles were sending her body.

They drew surprisingly few looks inside the hospital itself. Chris was sitting up in bed, his eyes glued to the cartoon show on the television set on the wall. The remains of his breakfast were on a tray, and only two of the other beds in the ward were occupied. One boy was asleep and the other one was absorbed in a different television show.

Chris started to smile when he saw Marly, but then he looked past her and must have seen Sam. The smile disappeared, replaced by a look of caution.

"Hi, Chris," she said.

"Hi."

"How are you feeling?"

"Okay, I guess."

Sam pulled a chair over close to the bed and indicated with a nod that Marly should sit. Grateful, she did, watching as Sam perched on the bottom edge of the hospital bed. He tilted back his battered hat in a gesture that had become very familiar to her.

"You gave us quite a scare, kid," he told the boy. "But you look a lot better now than you did yesterday. Still have a headache?"

Chris gave a small nod.

"Nice shiner," Sam said. "Zeke's nose is still swollen, too."

Chris touched his eye gingerly, but didn't look at Sam. Marly could see how nervous he was. "Why'd you run away, Chris?" she asked.

The boy didn't move.

"It's okay, kid. No one's gonna hurt you."

Chris looked up at Sam's words, and his eyes darted from one adult to the other, as if measuring the truth of their words.

"Your face has blood on it," he said timidly.

Sam touched a finger to his cheek. "So it does. Marly and I had a small accident."

"There's blood on your hand, too," the boy pointed out nervously.

"I told you it needed to be washed," Marly scolded.

"Women. They've always gotta nag a man," he said to Chris. The boy didn't smile back. "Okay, boss, I'll go wash up." He stood and disappeared inside the small bathroom. An aide appeared in the doorway a moment later to collect the breakfast tray.

"What kind of accident?" Chris asked suspiciously as soon as the woman left.

Marly debated about telling him the truth, but there

was an adult expectancy in his look. "It wasn't serious. The brakes failed on my truck. Sam was able to bring it to a stop in the grass."

Sam stepped from the bathroom. His face was washed. The small cuts were hardly noticeable, but he had wrapped his hand again, this time in a towel.

"Shortage of bandages in the bathroom," he explained when he saw her pointed stare, "but it doesn't need stitches." He sat back down at the end of the bed and faced the boy. "I need your help, Chris." He didn't whisper, yet his voice barely carried to where Marly sat. "Remember the night of the shooting?"

Instantly fear distorted the child's features. "No way, man. I told you I don't know what you're talking about."

Sam's expression remained unperturbed. "Officer Porterfield was killed last night. Seems like the feller who murdered him is trying to frame me for that killing, too."

"I don't know nothin'." Chris scooted backward until his spine came into contact with the headboard.

"Sam's in trouble, Chris," Marly protested. "You have to help him if you can."

"I don't know nothin'." He looked frantic, as if he wanted to scramble from the bed and flee down the hall. His lower lip trembled as his eyes darted about in search of safety. He kept shaking his head from side to side.

Sam reached out and patted his ankle. Chris jumped and pulled his leg away from the contact. His fear wrenched at her. Apparently it did the same to Sam.

"It's okay, Chris," he said softly. "I'll find another way to get help."

Marly didn't know whether to be glad or sorry Sam

wasn't pushing. Chris had been there the night Matt was killed. That much was obvious, but so was his terror.

"You don't have to be afraid of Officer Porterfield anymore, Chris," she told him.

"Marly..." Sam shook his head.

Chris, however, stared at her blankly.

"We know he killed the man in the park, but he can't hurt you anymore."

Instead of being reassured by her words, Chris swung his head from side to side. "No, he didn't." He clamped a hand over his mouth, his gray eyes wide with fear. "I don't know nothin'," he mumbled.

Marly's heart slammed against her chest. She didn't know what to say. Sam, however, stood and pulled her to her feet. When she was standing, he repositioned the chair. Chris never took his eyes from Sam.

"It's okay, kid. We're leaving. Just remember one thing. You don't have to always live on the streets. Marly tried to show you that there's other places, other ways you can live. All you gotta do is keep your nose clean, get an education, and work hard. Think about it."

"I can't tell you," Chris protested.

"I understand. I'll work it out. Take it easy, Chris."

Marly let Sam leave before she faced the boy. "If you can tell *me* what happened that night, call me. Okay, Chris? Anytime. You can even call me collect."

"I can't."

"Can you tell me why?"

Chris shook his head.

"Okay, honey. I'll call your aunt to check on you later."

She found Sam leaning against the door, his expression completely unreadable.

"Don't push him, Marly. He's scared."

"I know, but he was there. He knows something. Maybe if he thought we could protect him—"

"He knows better. Protect him how? From whom?"

"Sam, he said Porterfield didn't kill Matt."

"I heard him." They started toward the staircase.

"What does that mean?"

"That I picked the wrong offender?"

"I'm serious."

"So am I."

"Fine. How are we going to get home?" Marly asked as they headed down the stairs.

Sam didn't look at her. "*You're* going to call the farm and have Keefer or Lou come and pick you up."

"Not likely. What am I supposed to tell the police?"

"How about the truth? You lied last night, and we weren't together."

"Sam, let me help you."

He paused on the landing at the touch of her hand. Her lower lip was slightly puffy from the accident. There were circles under her eyes attesting to lost sleep. Her hair lay tangled and windblown, despite her efforts to push it back behind her ears. She was sweet and lovely and the most powerful temptation. "You already have."

He leaned toward her. Her lips were soft, warm, welcoming. He ran his tongue over the small swelling, but the taste of her was pure sin. She yielded so openly to the pressure of his tongue. He was hot and hard from that contact alone. She filled his senses, as well as his arms. A taste wasn't enough. Not nearly enough. He wanted more. He wanted it all. The realization brought him to his senses.

Marly stepped back as soon as his hands dropped to

his sides. She looked as stunned as he felt. The tip of her tongue probed her lower lip, as if tasting him there.

"Don't do that," he said, more sharply than he'd intended.

She tilted her head back and to the side as she studied him. "Does it bother you?"

"You know damn well it does."

"Good." She started down the last flight of stairs. "You've been bothering me ever since you set foot in my front yard, cowboy."

He started to respond, but found himself grinning instead. No wonder Rayback—Kramer—couldn't hang on to her. No mere mortal could capture all that fire. A man would be lucky if he could tame her just a bit. Very, very lucky.

She pulled open the door at the bottom and stepped into the main corridor. "What are you going to do now, Sam?"

His amusement faded as she introduced reality. "It's better that you don't know."

"Well, you can't go back to my place, that's for sure."

"No, I— Damn!" He grabbed her by the arm and dragged her back inside the landing.

"What's wrong?"

"Someone must have found your truck and called it in. Carter's out there, talking to some locals."

"Local what?"

"Police," he told her grimly. "At a guess, my cover is blown all to hell, and I suspect you're in almost as much trouble as I am."

Chapter Nine

"What are we going to do?"

He shook his head. "You're not going to do anything. I'm going to have to find another way out."

He turned and started down the basement steps, and she followed. "Will you stay put?" he asked.

"No. You'll need help."

"You can go to jail for aiding and abetting a fugitive." He stopped as he reached the bottom and cautiously opened the door onto another corridor.

"At least it will make my neighbors happy. Here. This way. There's an exit."

It was like trying to divert a freight train racing down the tracks. There was no way to deflect her short of physical force. Sam heaved an inward sigh. He could always claim he'd forced her to go with him.

He was relieved to find no police cars on this side of the building. They hurried outside.

"Take off your hat," she suggested. "It's too easy to spot."

"Good point." He clutched the hat to his churning stomach. "Over there." He pointed to a blue-and-white sign near the curb, some distance away.

"We're going to take a bus?"

"Would you rather steal a car?"

"Well, it would certainly be more exciting, but on the whole, the bus sounds safer—even if we are going to miss it."

As if hearing her words, the bus lumbered into sight and slowed to disgorge a passenger. They were too far away to catch it, but they began to run anyhow. The bus pulled away in a plume of exhaust.

"Damn. Looks like we steal a car, after all."

"Sam! Look out!"

A familiar red pickup truck careened around the corner, heading straight for them. Sam grabbed Marly and spun her around, out of its path, even as the vehicle leaped the curb and plunged onto the sidewalk, coming to a lurching halt only a few feet from where they stood.

Sam rushed forward, intent on mayhem.

"Hi, Sam. Hi, Marly." Hector's chubby eleven-year-old face peered around the cab of the truck. Emma's ashen features stared at him from behind the wheel. Zeke waved from the center seat, while Jerome jumped down from the passenger side.

Sam uttered a single oath, as he continued forward and pulled open the driver's door. "Emma, what the hell do you think you're doing?"

"We came to rescue you," Jerome told him. His face split in a wide grin as he ran around the front of the truck. Emma, looking terrified, only stared mutely.

"Emma?" Marly asked incredulously. "But you don't know how to drive."

"You can say that again," Sam muttered.

Marly didn't look at him. "What's going on?"

The kids piled from the vehicle and began speaking in a jumble of voices.

"We came to rescue you."

"Yeah, we heard Carter talking to Sam's boss."

"He said the police were gonna arrest you and Sam."

Sam cut in, his eyes zooming toward Emma. "The captain was at the farm?" Her tight curls bobbed once.

"I don't like him," Jerome said quietly.

"They were gonna take us all home," one of the boys announced. "Only, we don't want to go home." This statement was greeted by five raised voices, united in agreement.

Marly made a choking sound. Emma looked grim.

"I don't believe this," Sam muttered.

"Emma didn't have the key, so we had to help," one of the boys explained.

Mickey beamed with pride. "I know how to hot-wire. My brother showed me." Then he shrugged. "Only I can't drive a stick shift."

"Zeke knew how," Hector told them smugly, "but his feet don't reach."

"Besides, Emma wouldn't let him," Jerome put in.

"But I told her what to do," Zeke added cheerfully.

"Resourceful little monkeys, aren't they?" Sam said. Then his attention was drawn to the front of the building. "Marly, get in the truck," he ordered before she could respond. "You guys pile in the back. Move!"

Marly followed the path his gaze had taken. "Oh, sugar. Hurry, boys."

Two security guards started across the lawn in their direction. Marly raced around to get in beside Emma, who scooted over onto the middle seat. The kids scrambled into the bed of the truck, except for Jerome. He squeezed onto the front seat next to Emma. Sam started to protest, decided there wasn't time, and plopped his hat on Jerome's small head before sliding in beside the boy. With a casual wave to the men heading in their direction, he backed the truck off the sidewalk and made an illegal U-turn.

"What are we going to do?" Marly asked.

Sam flicked a glance at the rearview mirror. The security men stopped to watch, no doubt memorizing the license number. "I don't know. I'm thinking."

"Well, do it faster."

"Very funny. Is there a Metro station around here?"

"Not close. There's one in Rockville, and one on Shady Grove Road."

"Pick one and give me directions," he demanded as they reached the traffic light.

"Turn right." Marly issued instructions without further prompting. Emma didn't say a word.

"Why are we going to the Metro station?" Marly finally asked as he turned down a residential street.

"We need to disappear."

"With the boys?"

"Unless you want to leave them along the side of the road somewhere. After all, they did come to rescue us, right, Jerome?"

A huge grin beneath the impossibly large hat was his answer. Jerome removed the hat and held it in his lap. "Emma isn't a very good driver," he said.

Sam chuckled, and Emma nodded in agreement.

"Sam, how can you laugh about any of this?" Marly demanded.

"Tears aren't manly."

"Marly, don't be mad at Sam." Jerome squirmed a bit on the seat, finally pulling something from his pocket and leaning forward to look at Emma. "Should I give it to her now?"

At Emma's nod, he handed something to Marly.

"What's that?" Sam asked.

"The petty cash from the household fund," Marly said in a quiet voice. "Emma—"

The older woman's hand came out and closed over Marly's in a gesture of comfort.

"Smart thinking, Emma," Sam told her. "Money's important when you're on the run. Does my boss know I was working there?"

Emma nodded.

"Is he that mean guy who said he was your friend?" Jerome asked.

Sam's lips twitched. The captain had a gruff manner of speaking, even when he wasn't upset.

"He said they were gonna throw a book at you. And he yelled at Emma," Jerome added, highly incensed.

Sam grimaced. It had only been a matter of time before someone identified him. George might be a friend, but he was still the captain and he played by the rules. Bill's murder and Sam's proximity to it would be enough to make George start wondering about Sam's innocence. On the plus side, George was a good cop. He'd really probe into Bill's background now, and once he heard Chris's name, he'd know the boy needed protection. That was all to the good.

"What are we going to do once we reach the Metro?" Marly wanted to know.

"Are all the boys from D.C.?"

"Yes."

"Well, first we have to get them home, and we can't deliver them in this truck. The police will have an APB out on it any time now. Heck, we'll be lucky to make it to the Metro station without being stopped, with the boys riding in the back this way. It isn't safe."

"Uh, Sam... I don't think the subway stops in the areas where most of the boys live. I'm not even sure you can get a cab to go into some of their neighborhoods.''

He found he could still smile. ''We'll cross that bridge when we come to it.''

It didn't take long to reach the Metro stop at Shady Grove Road. Since it was a Saturday, Sam even found a parking space. Outside, he gathered the boys around him and wrote down their home addresses and telephone numbers on a pad Emma took from the glove compartment.

''But we don't want to go home,'' Donald protested. ''We want to stay with you and Marly.'' The others agreed.

''Unfortunately, if you stay with us, it will make it easier for the cops to find us. That's why we have to spread out.'' This was something they understood. ''How many of you have ever been to the zoo?''

''Sam!'' Marly's expression clearly stated that he, too, had lost his mind. ''We don't have time for that.''

''Sure we do. We'll go there first and have lunch.''

Over excited cheers, they started walking toward the Metrorail, Emma silent at their side.

''Are you insane?'' Marly hissed at him.

''No question about it,'' he told her cheerfully. Then, more quietly, he added, ''We need to get them safely home, and I need to buy us some time until I can figure out how to do it. I'd rather take them into D.C., someplace like the air and space museum, but I'd never get the gun past the metal detectors. The zoo's close to D.C. and doesn't have that kind of security.''

Marly muttered something that sounded like a plea for strength.

''Don't worry. If worse comes to worst, we'll send the boys to the security office at the zoo with a story about being lost. The park police will see to it the kids don't come to any harm until they can be returned to their parents."

"Uh-huh. Who's going to protect the zoo from them?"

Sam chuckled and gave her shoulder a gentle squeeze.

"Aren't we taking a big risk getting on the subway, Sam?" she asked.

"Wasn't it you who told me life's a risk?"

She slid her hand in his. "Point taken. Let's go look at the animals, fool."

They had the Metrorail car to themselves when they first boarded, but before they reached the Woodley Park station the car was packed with people. Sam felt the irritated stares of some passengers, mostly directed toward the noisy children, who were chattering excitedly. The boys were having a great time. For them, this was all one big adventure.

They took the escalator up to street level and began walking toward the zoo. The kids tumbled about like puppies, chattering, pushing, and generally behaving like the eleven-year-olds they were. Only Marly looked as tense as Sam felt. Her face was pinched with nerves, and she kept looking around as they walked down the street.

"Relax," he whispered.

"Easy for you to say. I keep waiting for someone to shout, 'Stop, police.'"

"Well, if they do, just remember, I forced you at gunpoint."

"I'll say no such thing."

"You will unless you want to go to jail," he said quietly. "This is a game for the boys, but you and

Emma and I know it isn't. Come on, there's a hot dog stand over there."

"You're not seriously going to eat one of those things, are you?"

"Anybody want a hot dog?" Sam called out.

Hot dogs, sodas and ice cream later, they finally made it inside the zoo itself. The park was crowded with families and kids of all ages. Sam worried that one of the boys might get separated from them, but Emma seemed to have a sixth sense about that, herding them together when they were tempted to stray.

A park policeman gave the group a hard look. Sam suspected it was because Hector was hanging on the fence, debating the merits of climbing over.

"Hector, stay off the fence," he scolded.

"If even one of these boys throws up, you're on cleanup detail," Marly threatened loudly, while the boys stared at a disinterested antelope. "I told you not to feed them all that junk food."

The policeman relaxed, and Sam grinned, wishing he could hug her. She had wonderful instincts. "Hey, they were hungry. Would you have preferred we take them to a public restaurant?"

"Not for money."

"Sam, come on!" Mickey shouted. "We want to go see the lions."

"I'm just telling you, if they get sick, you're in charge," Marly warned.

Sam caught the guard's eye and grinned unrepentantly. "Relax. They're kids. God made 'em with cast-iron stomachs."

"And the ability to create chaos out of thin air," Marly agreed.

The guard chuckled as they strolled past him.

Sam continued the conversation, taking Marly's hand. "Hey, they're good kids, they're fed, and they're stretching their legs. What more could you ask for?" He lowered his voice. "I need to find a phone booth and check on bus routes."

"We're taking them home by bus?" Marly asked quietly.

"My first thought was to send them home in a taxi, but you're right, I don't think you can pay enough to get one to drive Donald home."

Marly squeezed his hand. "They might if we went along and tipped generously."

He considered that. "How much money do you have?"

"Five hundred," Emma said, pausing in front of them.

Sam whistled. "That's some petty cash fund."

"You never know when there's going to be an emergency." Marly's expression showed no trace of humor.

"Hey, Emma, c'mere and lookit this," Zeke called. Emma cast them a serene smile and walked over to the group of kids crowded around the elephant enclosure.

Sam slipped an arm around Marly's shoulders. "Have I mentioned that I like the way your mind works? Among other things."

Startled out of her pensive mood, she blinked before giving him a slow, provocative smile. "No, but I like the sound of that. Being appreciated for my mind. How novel. It's also very seductive, Mr. Moore. Later on you'll have to tell me about those other things you like about me."

Only the boys and the crowds surrounding them kept him from pulling her into an embrace. He settled for squeezing her gently. "You confound me, woman."

"Good. I do try."

Sam threw back his head and laughed. She was utterly unpredictable, devastating to his senses, and loyal to the core. He'd never met anyone like her.

They decided to let the boys enjoy the animals for a while, content to stroll hand in hand as the kids moved from one exhibit to another. Even Emma seemed to be having a good time. Maybe it was dangerous to steal this moment, but Sam wanted to savor the little time he had left with Marly.

Two hours later, they sat at tables near the refreshment stand, sipping cold drinks. The boys were finally winding down. It was time to bring this sojourn to an end.

"What now?" Marly questioned. "There's a phone booth over there."

"Darn. Too bad I'm not a superman."

Marly rolled her eyes. Sam set his empty cup down on the table. "I've decided to use a cab, if we can find one that will take all eight of us," he said seriously.

"It will be a pretty tight squeeze, won't it?"

Emma raised her head. "I'll go."

"You mean alone?" Marly asked.

"Yes."

Sam studied the two women. "It's not necessary, Emma. We can all go."

She gave a shake of her head, sending her tightly permed curls swaying. "Dangerous."

He knew she was right. "Emma, the cops could charge you with aiding and abetting."

"No." Emma could sure pack a lot of explanations into one word. Her blue eyes sparkled in defiance of the very idea of her arrest. Sam would have protested, but Marly intervened.

"Emma can handle the police, Sam. She's just taking the boys home."

"After hot-wiring a truck..."

"It was my truck."

"...and helping two wanted fugitives escape."

"As her boss, I ordered her to accompany us and help us see that the boys were returned home safely before we agreed to turn ourselves in."

"But..."

Marly and Emma had identical looks of determination on their faces. Sam shut up. The two were in obvious agreement.

"Okay, ladies, what do you say we get this show on the road."

Marly finished her cola and watched Sam explain the plan to the boys. Naturally, they protested their return home, but Sam was wonderful with them, making it an exciting adventure and making each child feel important. She could love this man.

Sam and the boys were several steps in front of the women as they headed out of the zoo. Marly slipped Emma half the cash.

"No," the older woman protested.

"You'll need it for cab fare."

Emma nodded, frowning in concern. In exchange, she produced a credit card.

"What's this? I have—"

Emma's eyes willed her to take it. "It's mine."

And Marly understood. The card was in Emma's name. The police wouldn't be looking for that, if she and Sam needed to charge something. "You're so smart." She hugged the woman hard. "And a wonderful friend."

"Be careful."

"I will."

Cabs were plentiful. It didn't take Sam long to hail a driver who was quite willing to ride all over D.C.—for a price.

The man scanned the list of addresses and looked at Sam assessingly. "We've gotta cross zones."

Sam handed him a twenty. "I'll tip you up front. Our van was towed," he explained. "We have to recover it, but first we have to get the social worker's kids back home before the parents start screamin' for the cops."

"Okay. They can climb in."

Sam waved the boys over, and they began to crowd inside the vehicle. The kids were still pumped and full of chatter. Marly hugged each boy in turn, promising to call them and arrange for their return to the farm to finish their vacation. Jerome slipped his hand inside Sam's. The two had somehow bonded since their initial meeting in her front yard.

Sam dropped down to eye level with the boy on the dirty sidewalk. "Thanks, kid. You take care of yourself and stay out of trouble, okay? I'll come see you when I get clear."

Jerome nodded silently, his chocolate eyes brimming with unshed tears. "Bye, Sam." He wrapped his bony arms around Sam's shoulders and squeezed. Then he turned and clambered inside the cab next to Emma. Sam stood and Marly slipped her hand around his waist. They waved as the cab pulled away.

"You're a nice guy, Sam Moore."

"Actually, it's Joe Walker."

She tipped her head to study his face. "I'm going to have trouble with that. You'll always be Sam to me."

His smile was as warm as the sun on her face. "No problem. It's my middle name. My family called me

Sam when I was a kid, so I'm sort of used to it. Besides, I like the way you call me Sam."

"Good, because I'm a creature of habit."

His eyebrows arched. "Oh? Got any other habits I might enjoy?"

"One or two."

Sam flagged down another cab. "I want details as soon as we get five minutes alone. Union Station," he told the driver.

"Oh, it will take a lot longer than five minutes," Marly assured him. She savored the feel of his arm around her shoulders, and they rode in silence to the train station.

"Now what?" she asked as they strolled inside.

Sam gave a small shrug. "The Metro, where else?"

They took the red line to Friendship Heights without speaking, both lost in their own thoughts. Marly let Sam lead her onto the busy street. He obviously had a destination in mind.

"Is it a secret?" she asked.

"What?"

"Where we're going?"

He smiled contritely. "My partner has an apartment down the street."

"Is that wise?"

"It's a good neighborhood."

"I meant—" Then she saw that he'd been teasing.

He touched the tip of her nose with a finger. "I know what you meant. No, it's probably not wise to go there, but I'm fresh out of ideas. Besides, I asked him to run down a few leads for me. Maybe he'll have some information that will help."

"And maybe the police will be waiting there to arrest you."

All humor faded. "Lee won't turn me in."

"Aren't you setting him up as an accessory?"

That brought Sam to a complete halt. "Yeah. I am." He rubbed his jaw thoughtfully.

"Why don't we rent a motel room instead?"

Sam tilted back his hat, searching her face. It took fierce effort to keep her features from showing any emotion.

"Why, Marly, I didn't know you were that sort of woman."

"You want to know what sort of woman I am?" she inquired with a syrupy sweetness. "I'm the sort that requires a minimum of six hours of sleep out of every twenty-four. Otherwise I get cranky." She pushed a finger against the hard muscles of his chest. "Very, very cranky. You don't want to see me when I'm cranky, Sam. It isn't pretty."

The harsh lines on his face relaxed, his eyes crinkling at the corners. "Heaven forbid. I'm too used to seeing you look beautiful."

His words surprised her even as his hand came to rest against the small of her back. They ignored the crowds of people around them as they started walking. "There's a decent hotel down the street, over the Bethesda line. Think you can make it that far?"

In the sexiest voice she could carry off she responded, "Try me, cowboy."

A new tension was communicated by the pressure of his hand against her back, but he didn't break stride. "That's an offer I won't refuse, you know."

"I certainly hope not."

Marly swallowed, amazed at her brazen behavior, but she didn't regret her words. She wanted to be with Sam. He was wanted for the murder of her ex-husband, but

Sam hadn't murdered anyone, and she was going to help him prove it. She thought about ways and means. Sam's regular channels into the police department were closed to him, but maybe there was someone she could call to help. After all, the brotherhood of police usually extended to wives and widows. Maybe ex-wives counted, too.

"I guess we both need some rest," he said softly. "Right about now, I could use some of that liniment you gave me last night."

Until he spoke, she hadn't given much thought to her body's demands, but now she became aware that Sam was right. She was stiff and sore all over.

They strolled like lovers down the crowded street. As she had been all day, she was extremely conscious of the man at her side and the butterflies wreaking havoc on her nervous system. She hadn't slept with anyone except her husband, and not even him in the past year and a half, yet she and Sam would do more than just sleep once they got inside that motel room. Their attraction was too intense for it to be otherwise.

Matt had been a polished lover, extremely skilled in pleasing a partner, but when she found out about his first affair, it had killed something in her. A sense of her own power as a woman.

"Marly?"

She realized they had stopped walking. They were standing outside a motel, and Sam was studying her from beneath his battered Stetson with that penetrating gaze of his. His brown eyes were soft with questions emphasized by his words.

"We don't have to do this. We can go inside, and you can call Keefer or someone to come and get you. The police won't charge you with anything at this point. They'll give you a hard time, but—"

She rested a finger on his lips to silence his words. "You're a good man, Joe-Sam Walker."

He smiled.

"I think you'd better wait out here and let me register."

"Why?"

"Because I'm the one with the credit card."

Sam frowned. "Credit cards can be traced pretty quick."

"I know. So does Emma." Marly produced Emma's card.

His expression was stunned and then amused. "I think I love her."

"I know the feeling. Come on, cowboy. I can't hold back the yawns much longer." A blatant lie. The last thing she was thinking about was sleep, with Sam at her side.

Nerves sent her muddled thoughts spinning at the sight of the two beds dominating the small room. She looked at Sam. If she hadn't known better, she'd almost have said he looked as jittery as she felt. Was he having second thoughts about making love with her?

"Why don't I run down the street and pick us up a few things we'll need?" he said abruptly.

"Sam, you can take the other bed, if you don't want to sleep with me."

His expression was completely surprised. "Jeez, Marly, where did that come from?"

"You look uncomfortable. I just thought maybe I was pushing you into something you don't want."

He pulled her forward and slid his hands down her back, to cup her buttocks and pull her more tightly against him. Her body throbbed with life and awareness of the sensual heat of him.

"Does this put that idea to rest?" His arousal pressed against her through the material of her jeans. "I've wanted you since the moment I first saw you standing in that yard, facing down two angry kids and a knife. Everything that's happened since has only reinforced that, Marly."

He captured her lips, teasing them with the tip of his tongue. She leaned into him, opening her mouth for his entrance, but he teased her some more, entering and withdrawing again quickly.

"Don't," she managed to whisper. "I want to taste you."

His dark eyes were smoky. He drew back to study her face, and his brows furrowed. One hand reached out to trace her jaw. "Your skin is so smooth. I'm leaving marks."

"It's okay," she hurried to assure him.

"No." He reached up to run a hand over his ragged bristles. "Those aren't the sort of marks I want to leave on your body, Marly."

She warmed under the intensity of his look. "What sort of marks *do* you want to leave?"

His expression was pure sin. "Wait for me. I need to shave, and I need to do something about protection."

He stepped back before she could protest the loss of contact and opened the door.

"I'll be back," he told her.

She quaked in the aftermath of his kisses, staring at the closed door where he had been. Her hand traced the path his mouth had taken, finding her skin raw where his heavy beard had scraped.

He'd be back. And she'd be ready.

Marly stripped off her clothing, finding her muscles protesting every movement. In the bathroom mirror, she saw what she had expected. Bruises from the seat belt faintly marked her shoulder and chest. But the belt had done its job, and she and Sam were both alive, thanks to his skill behind the wheel.

She turned on the shower, found a plastic shower cap and stuffed her wild hair inside. "I should have gone with him to buy a hairbrush and some makeup," she told her foggy reflection.

The hot water felt unbelievably wonderful against her sore muscles. She indulged in the feel of the water sliding down her skin, pretending it was his hands, half hoping he would return and find her there and join her. Finally, she had no choice but to step from under the spray. A yawn surprised her as she began to towel off. Sam still wasn't back, but he would be.

She gathered her clothing, rinsing out the undergarments and hanging them to dry. Plain cotton, she thought in disgust. She had given up the fancy silks and pretty lace about the same time she gave up on her marriage. Was she about to make another mistake?

"No second thoughts, Marly."

It wasn't love, of course. She knew better. A chemical attraction was the reality between a man and a woman. An attraction that would fade after a while. This would be an affair. No expectations of happily-ever-after this time. Just a man and a woman and a basic need.

As she slid beneath the cool cotton sheets, she wondered what was taking him so long. Could someone have recognized him? Was he even now being arrested? She pushed the fear aside. He'd be back. He'd told her so. She trusted him.

Hours later, she awoke from a sensual dream with a

panicked sensation in her chest. She lay silent and inert, assessing the source of her fear.

A heavy weight lay across her legs. A faint spicy scent filled her nostrils. The hot air on the back of her neck came from the man in the bed with her, sound asleep at her side.

Sam had returned.

Careful not to wake him, she slipped out from under his leg and stood. In sleep, with his face freshly shaven and his hair still damp from a shower, he looked younger than she would have thought, and impossibly handsome. Sleep erased the lines of strain, but not the raw potency of the man himself.

Desire swept her. She hurried into the bathroom, catching a glimpse of the satisfied smile on her face. He'd come back and he'd shaved, and he hadn't chosen the spare bed.

On the counter she spotted several new toilet articles including a hairbrush and a toothbrush. She used both. Her wet undergarments had been moved from the shower stall. The cotton was still damp, so she rehung them, pausing to gaze at her image. The bruises were darker now, but the hairbrush left her hair gleaming under the fluorescent light, tumbling in waves about her shoulders. It was the best she could do. She shut off the light, opened the door and stepped quietly back inside the room. With the drapes pulled, it was almost dark. Sam hadn't moved at all.

Marly smiled fondly, thinking how badly he needed sleep. She wouldn't wake him—for now. She slid back under the covers with quiet stealth, but she turned on her side to face him. Both his eyes winked open, and she caught her breath.

"I thought I was gonna have to come in there after you," he drawled softly.

"You're awake."

He reached out with one hand to cup her jaw. "Perceptive of you."

Only then did she realize he was totally nude under that sheet. Nude, and fully aroused.

Chapter Ten

"I hope you haven't changed your mind," he said softly.

"Not a chance, cowboy. I thought you'd never get back."

He reached out to stroke the side of her face. "Always nice to be missed."

Tenderly Sam drew her mouth to his. The kiss was deep and warm, with a sweet passion he was helpless to resist. "You're wanton," he murmured as she sampled his neck and chest.

"Is that a complaint?"

He settled her more snugly in his embrace, so that he could toy with the nipple of her smooth breast. "Not a chance."

Her eyes fluttered shut, and he sought the sensitive skin of her neck with his lips. She was so responsive, arching to allow him access. Her quiver sent flames of excitement licking through him. He explored her further, rewarded to discover that she was wonderfully sensitive everywhere he touched with his fingers or his lips or his tongue.

She was not a passive partner, either. He loved the feel of her hands sweeping across his skin. She played with his chest hair and seemed to delight in the way his nipples would also harden when licked or sucked gently.

"No more," he protested, knowing he wouldn't last long under her delicate ministrations. "My turn."

"Not yet."

She was so eager, her face aglow with an enchanting passion. When she moved down his body, they discovered he was ticklish when touched in just the right places. Sam promptly retaliated, making her writhe against him in laughter.

The playfulness exploded into passion when she took his length between her fingers and began to explore. Sam bent to recapture the tip of one tempting breast with his mouth. He could barely contain himself at the feel of her hand clenched around him. He reached down to still her fingers.

"I won't be able to take things slow if you keep that up."

She lifted her head, her hair whispering against his skin. "A pun?"

He tried to smile, but was distracted by the delicious torture of her hand.

"Slow is for later," she whispered.

Sam groaned in pleasure. When he could take no more, he again sought the vulnerable skin of her neck and throat, then descended to lave her breasts with his tongue. As he drew the nipple into his mouth and sucked strongly, she cried out his name. She pulled him away and inched down to capture his mouth with her own.

He was on fire, sure he would explode with his need of her. His fingers traced the supple length of her body, lightly cupping the crisp curls that protected her most sensitive place. Her body stilled in anticipation. Eyes that were partly closed with passion fastened on his.

Deliberately holding her gaze, he touched her and delved within, plunging rapidly in imitation of the movements to come.

"Sam!" Her hand closed over the muscles of his forearm, and he stopped, smiling down at her.

"Slow is for later," he told her, using her own words to fan the flames. Then he touched her most susceptible point. Marly lifted upward, a cry of startled pleasure wrung from her lips.

"Come here," she said, tugging at him.

He knew his grin widened. "Is that an order, boss?"

Her eyes gleamed with answering amusement. Her hand closed around him once more. "You want orders, cowboy? I'll give you orders."

He was already straining with need when she began stroking him to a fever pitch. He couldn't take any more of this subtle torture. He needed her.

Sam paused only long enough to tear open the foil packet he had set on the nightstand. She watched with hungry eyes as he applied the condom, then reached for him again, helping him to straddle her flushed body.

"C'mere, cowboy," she whispered. "Let's see how well you ride."

His chuckle was low and husky. She was incredible. And, at the moment, infuriatingly in control. He had to force himself to let Marly set the pace. He wasn't sure he would last as her nimble fingers guided him into position. Sam strained with the effort to hold back when what he really wanted was to plunge himself inside her.

He had never wanted a union this badly. Had never felt such a sense of perfect rightness. For just a moment, he paused as their gazes locked. Her face softened in welcome. Slowly, with more care than he'd thought he could manage at this point, he entered her.

His breath caught on a groan at the hot, exquisite pleasure as her body enveloped him. Her eyes hazed with answering passion as he began to move, slowly at first, inciting sensations so exciting he could barely hold back.

"Now, cowboy!" Marly clasped his shoulders firmly, moving more quickly with him, in a rhythm as old as time and as new as life itself.

Sam battled for control. The fantastic sensations became too intense. Too vital. Her breath fanned his cheek even as her nails scored his back. She moved with him, faster, harder, deeper, until he' couldn't hold on. He reached between their bodies and touched her where they joined. Her eyes widened. She cried out, a soft cry of completion, only seconds before his world burst in a kaleidoscope of pleasure.

He lay over her for several minutes, unwilling to lose the remarkable perfection of the moment. After a few minutes, however, Marly shifted restlessly beneath his weight. He rolled to one side, tugging her slick body on top of his. He cradled her head against his shoulder while they basked drowsily in a connection so complete it stole his senses.

"At least you don't make love with that damn hat on," she breathed in his ear.

Laughter rumbled through his chest to fill the room.

HOURS LATER as Marly stepped into her skirt, she blinked in amazement. Her cowboy was gone. Sam stood in the bathroom doorway, transformed. He was every inch the cosmopolitan man-about-town. He could have walked into any fashionable party in downtown

Washington and caused a commotion while people tried to figure out who he was.

And she had thought he made a terrific cowboy.

"You clean up pretty good," she murmured.

He chuckled, and the sound caused surprising reactions in a body she had thought was more than satisfied.

"I'm glad I've got another name to call you by now," she continued, "because you sure don't look like Sam anymore. Except for the boots, of course."

He looked down at his dark, newly shined boots, poking out beneath the hem of his slacks, and gave her one of his devastating smiles. "So, who do I look like?"

Clean-shaven and dressed in a navy blazer over an open dress shirt with pleated slacks, he looked fantastic. Better than fantastic.

With a shake of her head, Marly looked away as she fastened the small gold belt around her waist and smoothed the gaily colored peasant skirt over her hips. "I don't think your ego needs any further inflating," she told him smartly.

"Well, you look lovely," he said. The sincerity in his tone jerked her head up again. "I'm glad the clothes I bought fit."

Unsure how to respond, she settled for a noncommittal "Mmm..." Sam's gaze lingered on her in a caress her skin could almost feel. The simple white blouse, the skirt and even the open-toed sandals fit amazingly well. "One might almost wonder how you know so much about women's sizes," she said in an effort to regain control of her wayward hormones.

His eyes twinkled. "I have an older sister about your size. She's a bossy little thing, too."

Marly tipped her head. "Runs in the family, does it?"

Sam laughed, opened a dresser drawer and produced

a small jewelry box. "Here. This isn't what I'd like to give you, but I know enough about women to know an outfit isn't complete without earrings and a necklace."

"Sam—"

"It's a thank-you, Marly. For believing in me."

She took the box, almost afraid to open it. Inside lay two crystal teardrop earrings and a matching pendant. They sparkled even in the bedroom's dim light.

"They're perfect," she told him softly. And they were. She'd been half-afraid of something expensive. These, however, she could accept. These she could wear with pleasure.

He helped her fasten the pendant and watched as she adjusted the earrings. "They sparkle. Just like you. Come on, lady, let's go eat before I decide to feast on something besides food."

She lowered her traitorous hands so that he wouldn't see how they trembled at his husky tone. Judging by his knowing look, she needn't have bothered. "I need food," she insisted primly.

Sam chuckled as he produced a pair of heavy-rimmed glasses.

"I didn't know you wore glasses."

"I don't." He handed them to her. They were plain glass, but as a disguise, they were amazingly effective. She returned them and watched as he put them on. Once again his appearance changed. From cover model to handsome professor with just that minor alteration. No. It was more than just the glasses. He had added a slight slump to his shoulders, as if he were someone used to poring over a desk. And he'd rumpled his hair slightly. Enough to cover the small scar on his forehead. The transformation was incredible.

"You're a tricky man, Mr. Moore."

"Walker," he corrected. "And thank you."

They ambled hand in hand for several blocks before they found a restaurant where the service would be quick and impersonal, providing them a degree of anonymity. Marly couldn't have said if the food was good or bad. She focused on Sam. He was intelligent, funny and perceptive. They shared many similar views, but their differences provided quirky fun.

Fun. She hadn't had fun in years. It was astounding to feel this carefree, when her life was tumbling in shambles around her. This cowboy knew how to work his magic on more than children. She was captivated and she knew it.

It wasn't until they were outside and several yards away from the restaurant that Sam punctured her pleasantly relaxed state with his words.

"I have to go see Lee. We need information."

"That's for sure."

"I'll drop you at the hotel."

Marly didn't break stride, but it was an effort to keep her voice even and matter-of-fact. "Are we going to waste time having this discussion all over again? We're in this together, cowboy."

Sam's expression was hard to read, but there was no trace of humor there. "I don't think they'll let us share a jail cell."

"Then we'd better not get caught, huh?"

After a moment, he squeezed her hand and stepped up the pace briskly. "I hope those sandals are comfortable."

"If not, you can carry me."

"That'll make us inconspicuous."

Lee lived in a high-rise apartment building with a security desk in the lobby. When a neighbor kindly held the door for them with a friendly smile, they bypassed the desk and took the stairs to the second floor.

"What if Lee isn't home?" Marly asked.

"We'll go inside and wait."

He rapped on a door in the somber hall. No one answered. Sam pulled out a small flat case and extracted an odd object.

"Do they teach you this in detective school?" she whispered.

"No." He started to insert the device in the lock, but then he stopped.

"What's wrong?"

He shook his head. "The door's already unlocked," he told her, so quietly she had to strain to make out the words.

He stepped away from the door, pushing her back as well. Then he reached inside his boot and removed his revolver. Marly didn't make a sound, but a sudden spurt of fear threatened to choke her.

She had seen vestiges of Sam's cop persona before. This, however, was the first time she had seen him completely in that role. It was scary. Just the businesslike way he held that gun terrified her.

"Wait." His word was a scant trace of sound. Marly pressed her back against the papered wall, feeling the chair rail pinch her hips. Sam flattened himself against the wall on the other side of the doorway and slowly pressed the door open with the palm of his empty hand.

She didn't breathe as he entered the apartment, nor did she try to move. When he disappeared, the door swung partially closed behind him. What was she supposed to do if she heard gunshots from inside? Her cloth purse would make a pitiful weapon. The question became moot a few minutes later, when Sam reopened the door and ushered her in.

"It's clean."

She looked pointedly at the broken picture frame near his feet. "That must be a male point of view."

"I meant there's no one else here. Someone trashed the place."

His words were simple truth. It was a nice, airy apartment, furnished in garage-sale odds and ends. Now those same odds and ends lay scattered about in malicious destruction. Cushions were flung to the floor. The movie posters that had served as pictures were off the wall, some broken, others simply leaning drunkenly against other furniture. Clothing and personal items littered the carpet.

"What were they looking for?" she asked.

"Good question."

"Do you think it had anything to do with us?"

Sam paused to consider. "I don't see how, but I hate coincidence. Someone was looking for something."

"The rest of the missing money from the evidence room?" She didn't know why she said the words, but Sam's face took on a stony expression. He didn't answer.

She stepped over a single sock and passed a table littered with books and the remains of a TV dinner.

"I can't tell if anything is missing. Lee didn't keep many personal effects after the divorce."

Marly heard the note of bitterness reflected in his tone. "So what do we do now?"

Sam shrugged. "We wait."

Being in this messy apartment was making her edgy. "Mind if I turn on the television? I want to get a news report."

"News isn't on again until ten. I don't plan to be here that long."

Marly switched on the set. "He has cable." She indicated the box on top of the television. "Channel eight is a local news station, and CNN will have national and international news. Then there's the weather station—"

"Stop it, Marly." He moved to stand in front of her. "What's wrong?"

"I don't know. I'm just feeling restless, I guess." She looked away from his rugged features to avoid the temptation of touching him. The flicker of the screen caught her attention. "Sam! That was Chris! They just showed Chris's picture on TV. Let me turn up the sound."

"Police are asking anyone with information to call this number..." the reporter was saying.

Marly made an exasperated sound.

"Are you sure it was Chris?" Sam asked.

"Positive. Why would they show Chris's picture unless something has happened to him?"

He didn't answer her directly. He didn't have to. Her fear was mirrored in his eyes. "How often do they repeat the news?"

"I'm not sure. Maybe every hour?"

"Then I guess we wait."

Marly perched on Lee's worn leather couch and began flipping channels.

"Is there another news station?" Sam asked.

She shook her head. "I was hoping to get a newsbreak on one of the other stations."

"I have a better idea." Sam disappeared and she heard him open a closet door. When he returned, he was holding a radio. "Let's see if we can find a news station on here."

Eventually they listened as a reporter calmly stated that Chris was missing. He had last been seen in his hospital room, talking to the two of them.

"They think he's with us!"

Sam's only response was to lean forward, his head tilted as he listened intently to the announcer.

The police had tracked their pickup truck to the Metro station, and wanted persons with any information about them, or the six boys traveling with them, to come forward.

"Don't they know by now that we sent the others home?"

"The police know." Sam switched everything off. "Come on. We aren't safe here. Someone at the hotel is bound to recognize us if they're flashing our pictures on the nightly news."

"But we don't know that they are."

"Simple deduction, Marly. Trust me, by now our pictures are going to be in every living room with a television set turned to the news. And, once they trace us to the hotel, it's only a logical jump to Lee's apartment. I hope you didn't leave anything behind in the motel that you need."

Marly shook her head. He started back down the hall toward the bedroom.

"What are you going to do?"

"Try and find Lee's spare keys."

"What for?"

"Transportation."

"Oh." Lee must have two cars.

"The keys aren't in Lee's bedroom," he told her a moment later. "I'll check the kitchen, then we're leaving without them."

Marly nodded. She moved to stand by the sliding

glass door and stared at the busy street below. There was no longer any pedestrian traffic, only a steady stream of cars.

Was Chris okay? And Emma and the other children... She wished she could call and at least know that they were all right. The person who'd been making the phone calls to her wouldn't have any reason to hurt the children now. Her youth program was history.

Marly moved to the table, staring blankly at the books spread across it while she considered their options.

"Got 'em," Sam announced. "Let's go."

But her eyes had focused on the page beneath her hand.

"Marly? What's wrong?"

She tried to swallow, only her mouth was too dry. Wordlessly she nodded to the open book. "I told you the average person wouldn't know how to tamper with the brakes."

Sam stared at the book on auto repair. It was open to a page on brake linings.

"No." The word was hollow. As empty as the expression on his face.

"Your theory about Porterfield and the missing money—would it still work if you substitute your friend Lee for Porterfield?"

MARLY STARED at the Harley-Davidson and the helmet Sam held out to her. Strands of hair whipped at her cheeks as she shook her head. "I'd rather steal a car."

"We're not stealing." Sam placed the helmet down over her wild mane of hair. "We're borrowing. From my good buddy." The acid in his last words was more effective than anything else would have been. Marly adjusted the helmet. Her heart ached in sympathy.

"He may be innocent, Sam."

"Don't you think I know that?" he snarled. His features softened. "Sorry. I've known Lee a long time. He's a friend."

The betrayal in his eyes hurt her soul.

"There's an explanation for that book," he stated grimly.

"Maybe we were *supposed* to find it."

A frown creased his forehead.

"I mean, he didn't tear up his own apartment. What if someone did it to cover up the fact they put the book there to implicate him? Maybe they put something else in the apartment. You *did* say only some of the money was recovered."

Sam uttered an expletive. "Come on. We'll talk about this later."

"Where are we going?"

"To ask some questions," he told her grimly.

She thought about pushing for a better answer, but decided to wait once she saw his expression. "I've never ridden a motorcycle before," she told him. "And I'm wearing a full skirt."

"I know. It was a bad choice, but there's no time to change it now. Hike up the skirt and tuck it in. We don't want it getting caught on anything."

"I don't think this is a good idea, Sam."

"Pretend it's a short horse and don't argue. We're under a surveillance camera."

"Oh, my God." She barely resisted the urge to look around. He got on the bike and helped her straddle the wide machine awkwardly. Tucking in the voluminous skirt took several minutes. She was very conscious of the extent of bare leg that showed. So, she noticed, was Sam.

"You're going to stop traffic," he muttered.

"Thank you," she said sarcastically. "Just remember, this was your idea."

"Uh-huh. Put your arms around my waist and hold on tight."

"Where have I heard that before?"

He spared her a lopsided grin, and she gripped his waist as directed, then flinched when he started the noisy beast. She'd take a horse any day over this contraption. At least their emissions made the grass grow.

"How are you going to get through the security gate?" she yelled over the roar of the engine.

"No problem. Watch."

It was open. Sam must have noticed that fact earlier. No doubt he would have gotten them out somehow, even if the gate had been closed.

She clutched him tightly, amazed once again by his whipcord strength. It didn't take her long to adapt to the pattern of their motions. She automatically leaned with Sam as he steered the bike through the heavy traffic. This new rhythm was unexpectedly sensual. She pressed more closely against his back, savoring the play of his muscles beneath her fingertips.

When they stopped at a long traffic light, she took the opportunity to stuff the bulk of her hair under the helmet. They were drawing more than a couple of looks from passing motorists, and no wonder. Their outfits were incongruous with their mode of transportation. At least the visors on their helmets were opaque. Marly felt confident that no one they passed connected them to the wanted criminals being displayed on the area's television screens tonight.

Sam headed away from the main roads as soon as he could. Dusk dwindled to an evening sky and finally yielded to blessed darkness. Her tension increased with every mile they put behind them, because their destination was obvious to her now.

Surely the police would still be at the farm. If not, wouldn't they have left a guard or something? For certain, her men had been told to call if she returned. Either way, Sam could hardly drive straight into the yard on this noisy bike. It would draw every person in the vicinity right to them.

As though sharing her thoughts, he rode past the turnoff to the farm's main driveway without slowing and continued down the road. The noise of the bike prevented her asking the questions hovering on her lips. Then, without warning, he began to slow. They were in front of her west pasture when Sam pulled off the road into some tall grass and stopped.

"What are you doing?" she asked when he cut the engine.

"I thought we'd go across the field."

Marly eyed the pasture before them and thought about her open sandals. She'd have an uncomfortable hike in these shoes. "Why don't we—?"

"Do any of your horses come when you call?" he asked before she could finish.

"What?"

She followed the direction of his nod and saw a lone horse standing several yards away.

"Forget it." Even in the darkness, she recognized the animal. "That's Dickens."

"As in Charles?"

"As in filled with," she corrected. "He wasn't a very cooperative saddle horse before he and the barbed wire came into contact. Now…" She gave a careless shrug. "Carter wanted to destroy him, but I just couldn't do it. Where are you going?"

Sam stepped off the bike, walked over to the fence and climbed up to sit on the top rail. Dickens lifted his head. Sam made a soft, beckoning noise. The horse stamped its hoof and snorted in reply.

Marly stood in the grass, feeling wobbly after the ride, and grateful for the feel of solid ground beneath her feet. Riding a motorcycle was an interesting experience, but a car would have been a lot more comfortable.

Sam whistled. At first, Dickens shied nervously away. Moments later the horse was working his way closer to where Sam sat.

"This is a waste of time," she told him quietly as she moved to stand alongside him. "We'll never be able to ride him, even if you do get him to come over here."

"You never know until you try," Sam answered. "Right, Dickens?"

The horse trotted away, then turned and raced back, this time coming much closer.

"I'm not exactly anxious to get thrown," she told Sam.

"Dickens won't throw us, will you, boy?"

Dickens snorted in answer and tossed his head.

"I take that as a yes, Sam."

Sam ignored her and made a whickering noise. Dickens minced closer. Amazingly, he allowed Sam to stroke his muzzle before racing away again.

"Do we have time for this?" she asked.

"Sure. We want the bunkhouse and its occupants to settle down for the evening."

"What if the police posted a guard?"

"We want him to settle down, too."

Marly watched in a combination of awe and amusement as Sam coaxed the horse back over to the fence, where he allowed a few soft caresses. Sam talked quietly to the animal. She could have sworn the horse was listening. She was almost as startled as Dickens when Sam suddenly found an opportunity and swung himself onto the animal's bare back.

Dickens kicked out in shock, snorting in angry protest. Seconds later, Sam landed in the field on his back, a stunned expression on his face as Dickens raced away. By the time she reached his side, Sam was already getting to his feet, a chagrined expression having replaced his surprise.

"Now can we walk?" Marly asked.

"Not a chance. I should have grabbed his halter instead of his mane."

"You're determined to do this, aren't you?"

"Hey, it's a matter of pride." He dusted off the seat of his slacks.

"Uh-huh. Well, unless you've got some rope hidden on that motorcycle to make a neck lead, there's no way we're going to ride Dickens."

"Damn."

"Why don't we go in the back way?"

Chapter Eleven

Sam's mouth dropped in surprise. "What back way?"

"The road that leads to the bunkhouse."

"Why the hell didn't you tell me there was another way in?"

"When did you bother to ask?" she replied sweetly.

Thunderclouds crossed his face and were quickly dispelled by a rueful chuckle. "I guess I did sort of take over and start giving orders, didn't I?"

"You certainly tried."

Grinning, Sam gave her a quick hug and helped her back over the fence. "Okay, boss, I'm suitably chastised now. You want to tell me how to get to this back road?"

"Sure, but we can't just ride up to the bunkhouse on the motorcycle, Sam. Not unless you want everyone to know we're here."

"Is it a long driveway?"

"Longer than the main entrance, and more twisty, but sound carries at night. This is the country, remember?"

"Okay, we'll hide the bike and walk."

Marly looked down the empty stretch of roadway. "There's some heavy shrubbery near the mouth of the driveway."

"Good. Let's go."

The side road was really more of a dirt lane than anything else. The opening was heavily overgrown, and badly in need of another truckload of gravel. Carter hadn't told her the entrance was in such bad shape, and Marly hadn't had any reason to use it in a long while. She mused over Carter's failing while Sam hid the bike in a thicket of weeds.

"Give me your hand," he directed as they resumed walking.

"You romantic devil, you. A stroll in the moonlight?"

His smile was devastating. "Too bad we forgot the champagne," he quipped.

"No cups."

He tipped his head. "I could drink from your slipper."

"Now that I'd like to see."

They both glanced down at her open-toed sandals, and Sam laughed. He had a nice laugh. Warm and rich. Holding his hand was stirring some urges best left for later. Much later.

"Sam, I've been thinking."

"Uh-oh."

She ignored his teasing to blurt out the idea that had been tickling the back of her mind during their ride here. "What if Matt wasn't killed because he was a cop?"

Sam stopped walking. "What are you talking about?"

A shiver of apprehension traveled up her spine. "Didn't you say Lee was divorced?"

"What does that have to do with—?"

Marly could see his mind working in the new direction. "I know you don't want your friend to be guilty of murder, and neither do I. But Matt was... Let's just say he found women a challenge. He didn't care if they were single or married. He didn't even seem to care what they looked like. He just…he could be so damn charming. I mean, I wondered if Lee's ex-wife might have been one of his conquests."

Sam dropped her hand. His eyes had a contemplative, unfocused look to them. "Lee never said exactly why they divorced."

She could almost feel his mind turning over the possibility. Then he shook his head.

"That wouldn't explain the money that was stolen from the evidence room. Lee is not a thief."

He said the last with more intensity. Interesting. He could believe Lee was a murderer, but not a thief? Or did he just think Lee might be that passionate about his former wife?

"What if Porterfield was the thief? What if he stole the money, and someone else killed Matt?"

Sam muttered something under his breath. Marly plunged ahead. "Think about it, Sam. Porterfield knows he made a mistake. He's sitting there holding money from the evidence room when he learns Matt's a cop. Then Matt is murdered. He has to get rid of the money, so he spreads it around. Some in your place. Some in Lee's. Probably your captain and that other cop—Silvers?—their houses too." The more she thought about it, the more sense it made.

"Then who murdered Bill?"

"Maybe whoever was going to hang the goat. Maybe that murder had nothing to do with Matt's death at all."

Sam shook his head. "It's too complicated, Marly. I'm a cop. We like things nice and simple."

"Life is rarely simple."

"But murder usually is."

They started walking again, each lost in thought. Marly wasn't prepared to argue her case. She was only tossing out possibilities. Still, the more she thought about it—

"Do you know who Matt was sleeping with recently?" Sam asked.

"No." The thought of her ex-husband's infidelities had long ago ceased to matter on an emotional level. But a memory surfaced. "He got a phone call at the house the day he died. That was unusual. By then, most people knew not to call him there."

She thought back to the call. She'd been busy that morning, preparing rooms for the first group of kids. "It was a woman. She was pretty frantic to reach him. I told the investigating officers about the call at the time, but I had no idea what her name was, and they didn't seem very interested."

"Nothing distinctive about the voice? An accent? Deep pitch?"

"Nope. It was just a woman's voice, sounding strident. Was there something memorable in the way Lee's wife spoke?"

"No."

They lapsed back into silence and continued walking. Marly's thoughts sheared off into a whole new direction. "Sam, do you think Chris is in danger?"

"Hard to say."

"You're prevaricating."

"What do you want me to say, Marly? I'm as worried about the boy as you are." She felt his shoulders lift and fall in a shrug. "Unfortunately, I don't have a clue as to what might have happened, unless George recognized the name and spirited him out of the hospital to keep him safe."

"Then why would the press say he's missing?"

"It could be they're trying to draw me out."

Marly thought about that and shook her head. "I wish I could believe that."

"Yeah. Me, too."

"Do you think Jake was making the calls to me?"

"Or Carter."

That surprised her. "Why Carter?"

"He's in love with you."

Marly came to a stop, trying to read his face in the darkness. "No," she stated. "Carter's in love with the idea of getting partial control of my horse farm. I told you, we had a talk on the drive back from the hospital the other day. He asked me to marry him. I told him no."

"And you think that's the end of it?"

"I made my lack of interest pretty clear." She frowned. "Besides, why would he have done anything to jeopardize what he saw as his potential future by threatening me?"

"You have a different take on the man than I do," Sam told her as he stepped up their pace.

She wished he would take her hand again. She missed that innocent contact.

"Don't you think Carter was the tiniest bit upset by all the time you spent with the boys?" Sam asked. "Time he might think was better spent on himself and the horses?"

"That sounds more like Jake." But a thread of doubt hung suspended with her words. Carter *had* urged her to stop the program after her divorce went through. He'd wanted her to wait a year. On the other hand, Jake had made no bones about how much he disliked the "brats," as he called them. Yet he had risked his life in the well to help her rescue Chris.

"The point is, Marly, I don't trust anyone here except Emma."

"Well, thank goodness you don't suspect her, too."

"It was a man in that hayloft," he told her. "And I think it took a man's strength to kill Bill with that pitchfork. On the other hand, she could be working with one of the men."

"Now you're being ridiculous."

"Cautious, suspicious, careful even, but never ridiculous. Someone killed Rayback and Porterfield. Someone set fire to your barn and tampered with your brakes."

"Couldn't Lee have done all that?"

There was a beat of silence. "Yeah. Maybe."

Her hand reached to capture his again. She squeezed gently, and he returned the pressure. "So who do we trust?"

"Just you and me, kid."

"Sam, what are we doing back here?"

She sensed, rather than saw, his hand go to his jaw to rub it tiredly. "I want to talk to Emma, if she's here."

"Why?"

"Because I doubt that much goes on around here she doesn't know about. There may be things she knows or suspects about your husband that she never told you."

"But—"

"Shhh…"

They had reached the clearing at the top of the driveway. Sam paused, bringing Marly to a halt, as well. Stretched before them was nothing remotely resembling cover. Four vehicles were parked off to one side.

Sam realized he had never been inside the bunkhouse,

much less on this side of the building. The converted stable blazed with lights, and there were distinct movements behind one of the windows.

He hesitated, muttering a soft oath. They would never get across that expanse of open ground undetected.

"This way," Marly whispered.

He followed her to the right as she hugged the tree line, moving toward the training ring. Her white blouse was a beacon in the moonlight. Sam fervently hoped no one was watching as they moved from the shelter of the trees, leaving themselves exposed to prying eyes. The barn lay dead ahead, dark and silent. There was no sign of light or motion from inside that building.

The house stood to their left, equally silent and dark. Almost sinister in the moonlight. Sullen windows eyed their approach. Sam didn't like this. They were too exposed.

The moon whisked in and out among the low scudding clouds, but there was plenty of light to be seen by. Was anyone watching? The yellow tape marking off the barn sagged, an ugly reminder of their current situation. There was no sign of police activity.

"No lights inside the house." Sam spoke softly, his eyes never still as he surveyed the landscape.

"Emma's rooms are in the back, over there on the left. We can't see them from here. She's probably locked down the house for the night."

"Is there an outside entrance to her wing?"

Marly shook her head. "She uses the patio door on the porch or the front door. The front's our best bet. If we try for the patio door, we'll be in plain view of the bunkhouse. One of the guys might call the cops, thinking we're burglars."

Sam bent and retrieved the gun from his boot. He felt

Marly stiffen, but she didn't protest. "Let me scout it out first."

"No way. You aren't leaving me here alone."

He turned at the steel underlying her words.

"I'm afraid of the dark," she added with heavy sarcasm.

He bit back a comment. If Marly was afraid of anything, he had yet to see proof. One thing he knew for certain, she was stubborn. He would only be wasting time if he argued with her.

"Okay, but stay behind me."

She managed a withering look. He knew he was being bossy again, but surely she could see that this was different.

"No problem," she said drolly. "*I'm* not bullet-proof."

"Cute."

He decided the best approach was to walk straight up to the front door. Since there was no cover, they would be clearly visible no matter what they did. A direct approach wouldn't be expected.

He set off briskly, aware of Marly at his heels. The side yard was as silent as death. Not a great thought to have at the moment. Why the heck didn't she have dogs? At least barn cats? He'd have to remember to ask her about that one of these days.

Only when they reached the corner of the house unharmed did he relax a fraction. He paused to look and listen. The night seemed to hold a thousand eyes—all of them directed right at him. He couldn't shake a growing sensation that they weren't alone out here.

Moving more quickly now, he followed the porch around to the front. Sam kept a close eye on the barn, though he would have sworn it was empty. They mounted the steps and paused outside the front door.

Marly shifted silently. She, too, scanned the area. Did she sense another presence, as well? Seconds passed, but the night remained unruffled.

His curse was a breath of air. Marly nudged his empty hand, and he found her offering her house key. She held it so that the other keys didn't jingle together. He wanted to hug her and tell how terrific she was. He'd worked with professional backup who didn't have her innate common sense.

Sam wished like hell they'd met at any other time and place. He wished he could take her back to bed and make love to her until they were both exhausted—somewhere safe, where murder was something she only read about in the newspaper. Instead, he took the key and inserted it into the lock.

The foyer was another well of midnight. Nerves prickling, he stepped inside, gun first. He moved past the stairs to peer down the hall. A weak beam of light embraced the opening of the kitchen doorway, but there wasn't a sound from within.

Marly entered the hall and silently closed the front door. She waited motionless, ready to take her cue from him.

He would not let anyone hurt this woman.

Motioning to her to stay put, he started toward the light. Suddenly, the kitchen opening was blocked by a short, rotund figure. Only training and good reflexes kept him from pulling the trigger.

"Good. Come." Emma's whisper carried easily. She stepped back, out of sight. Sam moved cautiously, aware of Marly at his heels. As the soft yellow light grew brighter, he saw that it came from the door leading to Emma's suite.

They entered her sitting room, a cozy private chamber with all the amenities of a small apartment. Emma eyed the weapon in his hand and nodded bleakly. Sam tucked it in his waistband, watching as Marly stepped forward to give the older woman a tight hug.

"Chris is there," Emma said gesturing toward her bedroom.

"Chris is here? At the house?"

Marly sounded astonished. Sam found he wasn't even surprised. He opened the bedroom door and stopped. The spotless room appeared empty. "Chris?"

Blond hair jutted up over the edge of the bed. "Sam?" The youngster started to stand, but paused, looking puzzled and unsure.

Sam reached up and pulled off the forgotten glasses. "It's me, kid," he drawled.

Chris scrambled around the double bed and launched himself into Sam's arms. The small body trembled against his chest. Sam hugged him tightly, relieved the child was all right. He looked up and caught Marly watching.

"You okay?" Sam asked the boy.

Chris stepped back and nodded. "I was scared," he admitted.

"Yeah. Me too, kid."

"Hi, Chris," Marly said.

The boy moved to share a hug with her as well. "Are you okay?" she asked.

"Uh-huh."

"Let's go in the other room and talk," Sam suggested.

Emma returned from the kitchen with a pitcher of

milk and slices of coconut cake. When she would have left, Marly held out a hand to stop her.

"You can stay, Emma."

The woman shook her tightly permed head, but gave the three of them a reassuring smile before entering her bedroom and shutting the door.

"How did you get here? Why'd you leave the hospital, Chris?" Marly asked. "Your mother must be worried sick."

Chris looked down at his knees and said nothing.

"Did it have anything to do with what happened the night I got shot, Chris?"

Gray eyes jerked up to meet Sam's, fear etched clearly in their depths. Slowly, the small head nodded.

"Can you tell me what you saw that night?"

Chris hesitated, looking from one face to another. Sam could almost taste his fear. But it was up to the boy now. He either trusted them or he didn't.

"I was looking for Jackie. My brother? I heard these two guys yelling at each other, so I hid so they wouldn't see me. The cop sounded mad and real scary, but I couldn't hear all the words. Then the other guy—the one with the white hair—he sort of laughed and said something that made the cop real mad."

"How did you know the man was a cop?"

The small shoulders lifted and fell. "He said so. The guy with the white hair told him to put the gun away, and the other guy said, 'You know better. I'm a cop. I'm just gonna shoot you.' I decided I'd better get out of there, so I started going back to the road when you showed up."

"Did they see you?" Sam asked.

The blond head bobbed once. "After he shot you, he came after me, but I hid until he went away. Then I found Jackie an' I told him. He said I shouldn't tell anyone else. He said no one would believe me an' I'd go to jail or else the cop would come after me and kill me, too. I thought you were dead." The last was offered quietly.

Sam swallowed at the images that came to mind. "It's okay, Chris. You did the right thing, getting out of there."

"Is Jackie your older brother?" Marly asked.

Even as Chris nodded, Sam remembered George telling him the boy and his brother had both been picked up that night.

"Your brother was doing something illegal, wasn't he?" Sam asked. Chris hung his head without answering. "It's not important, Chris. Did you see this cop at the hospital today? Is that why you ran away again?"

"Yeah."

His answer was spoken so softly, Sam almost missed it. The boy was clearly terrified. "Can you tell me what he looks like?"

"He was big," Chris said tentatively. "Like you."

Well, that fit. Lee was the same general height and build. But so were a lot of other people. "What color hair?"

"I don't know. Dark, I think. I didn't get a good look at him."

Sam pinched the bridge of his nose. "You were right to be scared. Did your brother see any of this?"

"No."

"If you didn't get a good look at him, how did you recognize the cop at the hospital?" Marly asked.

Chris shook his head. "I didn't *see* him. I just heard him talking to Carter, in the hall."

"You recognized his voice?" Sam asked in surprise.

"Uh-huh."

There was nothing particularly distinctive about Lee's voice, so what did that mean? Did Chris just have an ear for voices? Chris turned to Marly with a distressed expression before Sam could ask.

"I dropped Jerome's watch in your barn the other night," he confessed. "He really likes that watch. His dad gave it to him right before he died. Can you find it and get it back to him?"

Sam and Marly exchanged looks. The watch was sitting in an evidence bag at the local police headquarters.

"Sure, Chris. I'll see he gets it back," Marly promised.

"Good. I didn't mean to take it. I found it an' I was gonna give it back, only I forgot. And I didn't mean to set fire to your field, either. I'm not gonna smoke anymore, ever."

"That's good, Chris. I'm glad," she said patting his shoulder.

"What happened that night in the barn?" Sam asked.

Chris shrugged. "I was gonna hide in the loft until morning, but Carter and that mean cop came in. They were fighting."

"The cop who shot Rayback?" Sam asked, instantly alert.

"No. The one who comes out here all the time and yells at Marly."

"Duncan?" Marly supplied.

"Yeah. I don't like him."

"Neither does anyone else, Chris," Sam assured him. "Why were he and Carter fighting?"

"'Cause of the goat. That cop wanted Carter to kill it and stuff its head in a box, but Carter didn't want to."

An oath escaped his lips. Chris didn't even notice.

"Carter was the one who took the goat up in the loft the night you ran away?" Marly prodded gently.

"Uh-huh. I hid over near the other ladder until he left. That's when I dropped Jerome's watch. I figured I'd hide outside by the rocks instead, only I found the tunnel and fell down the hole and couldn't get back out."

A flicker of movement drew Sam's eyes toward the window that looked out over the backyard. The window was open, he realized. And someone was out there.

Marly followed his gaze, asking a silent question. Sam waved his hand, motioning her to keep talking. He brought out his gun and moved to the door leading into the kitchen.

"Why was Carter helping Officer Duncan?" he heard Marly ask. He didn't wait for the boy's answer. He opened the sliding glass door leading to the deck and stepped outside. The tall figure crouched beneath Emma's window jerked upright at the sound of the door and turned to flee.

Sam shoved the gun in his waistband and leaped off the deck. He brought down the other figure with a flying tackle his high school coach would have been proud of. They rolled in the dirt for only a few seconds before Sam got his gun free again and jabbed it under the man's chin. Carter stopped struggling, his eyes wide in the moonlight.

"Don't shoot!"

"Give me a reason."

"You're a cop. You can't shoot me in cold blood."

"Try again. Or weren't you listening back there? I don't have a thing to lose."

Carter swore. Sam could smell the sour scent of sweat

pouring off the foreman. Beads of it ran unchecked down his face. He hauled the man to his feet. "Back to the house."

As they stepped into the kitchen, Sam stopped abruptly. Emma stood in the doorway to her quarters, a businesslike revolver in her hands. It was pointed right at them.

In that instant, it crossed his mind that they had been seriously overlooking the silent housekeeper. "Emma?"

She lowered the barrel and stood back. Her eyes never left Carter.

Sam swallowed and shook his head. He was seeing villains under the carpeting. Emma was one of the good guys. Wasn't she? He nudged Carter forward. "Yours?" he asked, indicating the gun in her hand.

"Matt's."

Sam eyed the forty-five. Somehow, he didn't doubt the housekeeper could hit anything she fired at. He had a feeling Carter had the same impression. "I'm just inviting our foreman here to join the party."

She stepped back, allowing them to pass. Sam felt certain that if the other man moved in a direction she didn't like, Emma would point the business end of that weapon right at his midsection again. Carter skirted her as much as he could, stepping inside the small sitting room and heading straight for Marly.

"Hold it, Carter," Sam barked. Marly had a protective arm around Chris, and she wisely tugged him back out of reach, allowing an armchair to come between them and her foreman.

Carter stopped. Emma brought the weapon up again, sighting it for good measure.

"For God's sake, I wasn't going to hurt anyone.

Marly, you know me. Tell them to put those things away."

Marly's hair swung in the lamplight as she shook her head. "I don't think so, Carter." Her clipped tone took the starch right out of him.

"Sit down," Sam ordered.

Carter slumped into the nearest chair and stared at Marly. "I only helped Duncan because of you."

"Pardon me if I can't find appropriate thanks."

"It's the truth. When Johnny offered me money to play a few pranks and make a couple of calls, I agreed. I thought you would turn to me for help. I want to marry you," he whined, but his fear was evident in the shifting of his eyes.

"Hell of a wedding present," Sam muttered. "A sacrificial goat and a hurt little boy."

"I didn't hurt any of the kids! I wouldn't do that. And I wasn't going to kill the goat, either. I told Johnny that. He was crazy. He was so pissed off because of her husband, he could hardly think straight."

"What does Matt have to do with anything?"

"Didn't you know? He was sleeping with Duncan's wife every chance he got." Carter turned his gaze to Marly.

There had been a time, long ago, when those words would have hurt. Now, all Marly felt was annoyed. "What do Matt's sexual conquests have to do with me?" she demanded.

Carter shrugged, but he kept his wary eyes on Sam. "Duncan hated Matt. He hates everything connected with this place. He blamed your youth program for the fact his kids got into trouble last year."

"Does he hate her enough to kill Porterfield?" Sam questioned.

Carter jerked in surprise. "No! Why would he do that? I thought *you* killed him."

"Sam didn't kill anyone," Marly stated angrily.

Carter looked pointedly at the gun in Sam's hand, his fear obvious. "Well, I sure didn't have anything to do with it."

"Do you think Duncan killed Porterfield?" she asked Sam.

"What would he have to gain?"

"He's a cop," Carter protested.

"So am I, but you're willing to believe me guilty of murder," Sam pointed out.

Carter swallowed nervously. He looked at the gun, and his eyes shifted to Marly. "Look, this is all a mistake. I was just trying to help you, Marly. You have to believe me."

Sam made a rude noise. Carter flinched. He wiped at a bead of sweat that trickled into his left eye.

"I figured if I could get you to dump the youth program you'd spend more time on the horse farm. I could build this farm into a showplace. I wouldn't cheat on you like Matt did, and I wouldn't be sidetracked by some outside job. We could have it all."

"Pretty brave words for a man on the other end of a gun," Sam said. But he had to admit that, though Carter was obviously scared, his words rang with sincerity.

"You really believed that?" Marly asked.

Carter's eyes lit with hope. "Sure. We can still work things out. I can forgive you for sleeping with him—" he nodded in Sam's direction "—and after he's gone we'll build the farm into—"

"You're fired, Carter," Marly told him.

His mouth dropped open in shock.

"Did you call the police when you realized we were here tonight?"

His eyes shifted restlessly once more as he struggled for words.

"Of course he did." Sam uttered an oath. "Emma, have you got any rope or—"

"Those cords we bought to fix the drape rod should work, Emma. I'll get them," Marly offered, but Emma bustled away, returning minutes later with two packages of cord.

"Are you going to kill me?" Carter whimpered.

Sam handed Marly his gun without a word. "Keep it pointed at him. Squeeze the trigger if he moves. Hands behind your back, Carter."

Carter swallowed hard, looking from one face to the other. "What are you going to do?" His voice cracked in fear.

"Truss you up and lock you in the bathroom," Sam told him. "Now turn around."

"I won't."

"Then I guess we'll just have to shoot you," Sam said with an easy nonchalance.

Emma brought up her gun, stopping Carter's forward motion.

"Hurry, Sam," Marly urged.

Carter looked stricken as Sam bound his wrists with a speed that amazed her. All the fight seemed to have gone out of the foreman.

"Into the bathroom," Sam ordered.

Carter cursed. "It won't do you any good. You're too late, you know. Duncan's probably already here."

"In that case," Marly replied, "I'll give Emma a raise if she shoots you before I do."

"Sam?" Chris stopped them outside the bathroom

door. "Someone just opened the front door," he whispered, eyes wide with fear.

"Johnny D.! Back here!" Carter yelled.

Chapter Twelve

"Marly, get the others out the bedroom window."

Sam gave Carter a hard shove, sending him sprawling into the small bathroom. As the door closed, Sam whirled around and Marly thrust the gun into his hand. She was already herding Chris and Emma into the bedroom. They could plainly hear the sounds of someone running in their direction.

Sam muttered a curse. With an apologetic look at the women, he fired the gun into the ceiling. The footsteps stopped. Everything stopped. Marly turned back to him with a shocked expression. Chris looked terrified. Only Emma nodded. She grabbed Chris by the hand and continued on into her bedroom.

"Go," Sam whispered to Marly.

After a moment's hesitation, she followed Emma.

"Carter?"

The voice that called out clearly belonged to Duncan.

"Stay where you are, Duncan," Sam warned.

"Walker?"

Sam placed him inside the kitchen. If he was following procedure, he'd be standing with his back against the wall, outside the door, ready to storm the room.

"I'm armed, Duncan. Not an easy target, like Porterfield was."

"What are you talking about? *You* killed Porterfield."

"It won't work, Duncan. Your buddy in here did some talking. We know all about your wife and the pranks and calls. Even the goat. With a little research, we should be able to nail you for Matt Kramer's murder."

"You're out of your mind."

"You want to come through the doorway and find out just how crazy I am, Duncan?"

Sam yanked the overstuffed chair around, placing it between him and the bedroom door. From behind it, he could cover the hall if Carter left the bathroom and the main entrance to Emma's apartment at the same time. All he had to do was sit tight and buy Marly some time. She would be smart enough to get Chris away and call for help.

"I've called for backup, Walker."

"Really? Not your usual style, is it? You're a hotdogger."

Sam knew Duncan hadn't killed Matt Kramer. Chris would have known if he was the cop at the scene that night. But Sam wasn't so sure about Bill Porterfield. Marly might have been right. Maybe they were dealing with two different murderers.

"Look, Walker. What do you say we make a deal? I'll let you go if you send your hostages out unharmed."

Interesting.

"Why'd you kill Porterfield, Duncan? Did he catch you in the barn that night? Was it an accident?"

"You're outta your mind," Duncan snarled.

Well, he couldn't dispute that comment at the moment.

"I thought it was strange when you showed up so quickly after we found the body," Sam continued. He glanced over his shoulder at the bedroom. The window was open, and so was the gun case against the far wall. The bedroom itself was empty. He smiled in satisfaction.

"I was coming home from a poker game with some fellow officers when I heard the call," Duncan said.

Duncan's voice now sounded muffled. Sam knew his time was up. "Great alibi. Was Kramer sleeping with their wives, too?"

Sam stood, raced into the bedroom, and climbed through the window. It was a short drop to the ground. He ran along the side of the house toward the front. Duncan's cruiser was parked at an angle across the driveway. As he hesitated, Sam saw three shadows move inside it. Suddenly the engine started up.

With a dry chuckle, he ran around to the driver's side. Chris beamed up at him as he slid inside.

"I saw his keys in the ignition," he told Sam proudly.

Sam grinned. "Remind me to thank him later."

Marly shoved something that looked suspiciously like a small automatic into the pocket of her skirt as he threw the car into gear and tore off down the driveway.

"Are you okay?" she asked before he could question her.

"Yeah. Sorry about the hole in your ceiling."

"I'll take damages out of your paycheck," she promised.

Chris clambered into the back seat with Emma as Sam turned the cruiser onto the main road.

"Can we turn on the lights and siren?" Chris asked hopefully, leaning back over the seat.

Sam released another chuckle, and Marly turned to ruffle his hair.

"Much as I'd like to oblige, kid, I don't think that would be wise at the moment. Maybe later."

"Put your seat belt on, Chris," Marly admonished. Then she turned to Sam. "Now what?"

"Now we turn ourselves in."

"No," Chris protested.

"It's okay, kid. This time we'll go to someone I can trust."

"You trusted Lee," Marly reminded him. "I have a better idea. Why don't we go to Matt's old boss? He's a nice guy, and he'd be a disinterested party. I know he'd help us."

"Is he married?"

Marly made a face.

"Sorry, love, but where your husband is concerned, I'm not real sure there are any disinterested parties around here. I can count on George to go by the book, even when he doesn't want to."

Emma made a soft grunt, and Sam saw her scowl in the rearview mirror.

"Look, gang, we're fresh out of choices here," he said in some exasperation. "At this point, we need protective custody. We've got enough information to send the investigators in several directions."

Marly tipped her head, disbelief clear on her features. "Yeah, but will they look, or will they just grab you and be satisfied?"

"Not with Chris here to tell them what he saw that night. What do you say, Chris? Will you help us?"

Chris looked solemn as he snuggled up against Emma. "Yeah. I guess."

"Thatta boy."

The radio spat a stream of unintelligible words. Marly lifted her eyes in question.

"The dispatcher is requesting backup. Duncan phoned in and reported his car stolen."

"Is he gonna get in trouble?" Chris asked.

"Yeah."

"Good."

Marly smiled and heard Sam cough to cover up a laugh. "So, where are we going? The Metro station again?" she asked.

Sam shook his head. "I don't think so. I need to find a telephone."

Silence radiated through the car.

Marly spoke slowly, picking her way through her tangled thoughts. "Sam, out of the hundreds of troubled inner-city youths, why would Porterfield send Chris to my program?"

Sam muttered something pithy under his breath.

"If this was a mystery novel, I'd put it down right now," she continued. "There are too many coincidences for me. We know Porterfield didn't kill Matt, right, Chris?"

"Uh-huh."

"And we know Duncan didn't kill him, either."

Sam nodded. "It had to be whoever stole the stuff from the evidence room."

"Or we're dealing with separate crimes."

"You keep saying that."

"You don't listen."

"I'm listening, Marly. I just don't necessarily agree with you."

"Well, who does that leave us with, except Lee?"

Sam fell silent. He pinched the bridge of his nose in a tired gesture as they sped down the empty road.

"I'm tired of playing mouse to Lee's cat. Why can't we have a turn being the cat?" Marly caught Emma's approving expression as Sam flashed her a worried look.

"Now wait a minute—"

"Let's go get him, Sam. Let's turn the tables. Let's get Lee, and beat the truth out of him, if we have to. Then we'll call your captain. Your captain has to play by the rules, but we don't. Not anymore."

Sam braked for a red light and twisted to stare at her. His array of expressions was almost comical. "You're serious."

"Darn straight."

Suddenly he began to chuckle, and the chuckle soon became a full throated laugh.

"Did I ever tell you you're a bloodthirsty little thing?"

Marly lifted her chin. "Yes."

"Smart," Emma put in.

"She is that. Sorry, Emma. It looks like if we ever get out of this mess I'll have to marry her instead of you."

"Good." Emma sat back with a smug expression.

"Ha!" Marly said, conscious of the sparkle of excitement dancing through her stomach at his words. "What makes you think I'd have you?" He was only teasing, but the image hung in tantalizing clarity. Was she crazy? She was never going to get married again.

"I want to go beat up the bad guy," Chris announced.

"No way," Sam insisted. "We are not going after a probable murderer. We're going to get smart and do this by the book."

SAM RUBBED HIS EYES and stared through the glassed-in lobby doors of Lee's apartment building. He watched in resignation as Emma strode up to the front desk, where a bored-looking clerk stepped forward to greet her.

"I can't believe I let you talk me into this," Sam muttered.

"Emma will be fine."

"I don't even remember for sure that Kathryn is the first name of Lee's aunt."

"It doesn't matter. Lee will either tell the guard to send her up, or he'll come downstairs to see who Emma really is, and she'll tell him you're waiting outside with Chris—"

"And he'll tell the guard to call the police."

Marly shook her head. "With a cruiser sitting right here in plain sight? I don't think so. He'll come out here to investigate. You know he will. You said he would."

"I'm exhausted. I don't know what I'm saying anymore. This is a stupid plan. It will never work."

"Of course it will work."

"I must be out of my mind."

Emma left the desk and headed back outside alone. "See?"

Marly didn't respond.

"Not there," Emma announced, getting back inside the squad car.

Sam breathed a sigh of relief. "He's probably out looking for us."

"Does this mean we don't get to beat him up?" Chris asked.

"It means we do things my way," Sam told them.

"We can wait until he comes back."

Ignoring Marly's suggestion, Sam started the engine. "I'm calling George and turning all of us in."

"Are they gonna throw me in jail?" Chris asked in a troubled voice.

Marly turned quickly to reassure the boy. "Of course not, honey. The police will only ask you some questions. You have to tell them the truth. Then they'll keep you safe until they arrest Lee."

Sam's brows raised cynically, but before she could remonstrate with him, Chris said, "I wish all cops were like Sam."

"Me, too," she agreed.

"Thanks for the vote of confidence, kid."

Marly frowned at Sam. "Most cops are good, caring people, honey."

"My brother says you can't trust nobody."

His brother was probably wise beyond his years.

"We'll just have to trust my captain," Sam stated. "Let George set a trap for Lee."

"I don't trust George," Marly protested.

"You don't know George."

"He's a cop."

"So am I. Despite this situation, didn't you just tell Chris most cops are the good guys?"

"Intellectually, I know that. The reality is, like Chris, I don't trust anybody associated with you right now."

"I'm too tired for this argument."

When Sam turned onto a residential side street, Marly tried to uncurl her fingers. He pulled into a parking lot behind a church, drove down to the bottom of the lot and backed the car against a line of bushes and evergreen trees. They were in the darkest corner of the parking lot, facing outward.

"What are you doing?"

"Keeping the car out of sight. There's a pay phone on the corner. I'm going to call George to pick us up."

She placed a hand on his forearm. "Are you sure about this?"

"Nope. But I think we're out of options, unless you've got a better idea."

"None you want to hear."

Sam leaned over, tilted her chin and placed a chaste kiss on her lips. "It'll work out. You'll see."

His hand stroked her cheek in a soft caress that brought a film of moisture to her eyes. She wished she could still believe in happily-ever-after endings. She watched him walk away with that long, sexy stride of his and felt an overpowering premonition of danger.

Chris yawned and Emma drew him against her body. She smiled at Marly and settled back against the seat, closing her own eyes. The stress factor was taking its toll. Maybe Sam was right. Maybe they were all too tired to think straight.

Minutes ticked past. Both Chris and Emma looked asleep. Marly shut her eyes, as well, and leaned her head back against the headrest.

Sam opened the car door a few minutes later, and Marly nearly screamed in surprise. "We're all set," he said quietly. "Hey, take it easy. Were you sleeping?"

"You've got to be kidding."

He turned on the ignition, and the radio crackled to life. Sam listened closely, then relaxed and turned the volume down low. He must have seen the question in her eyes, because he gestured toward the radio. "I want to make sure George doesn't decide to call for backup. If a call goes out or they switch to another frequency, I'll know we're being set up."

"Reassuring."

His grin was wide. "I thought so."

"Can you pick up D.C. police broadcasts from here? I thought we were still in Montgomery County."

"We are. If they're going to make a raid on us, they'll have to alert the locals, and we should hear about it."

"Oh."

He slid an arm around her shoulders and pulled her against his side. "Everything is going to be okay."

It was nice snuggling against Sam's body. There was a protected, cocoonlike feeling sitting in the darkness of the car, or there would have been if she could shake the sensation that they had overlooked something important. Sam lowered the windows, allowing the night sounds to add to this false sense of safety.

Marly rested her head on his shoulder as they sat there without talking. After a while, she let her eyes close again, wondering what would happen once Sam was cleared. He wouldn't just walk away from her, she was sure of that, but what sort of relationship did he want? For that matter, what did she want?

She was half-asleep when she felt Sam stiffen beside her. Her eyes popped open in time to see a long, dark car pull into the parking lot. It stopped and flashed its lights.

"Get down," he said quietly. "Let me make sure it's George. I don't want him to see you when I open the car door."

Heart pounding, she slid down on the seat as Sam opened the door, then shut it with quiet emphasis. She waited a few seconds before lifting her head enough to watch Sam step into the lights, his hands held away from his body. To keep from crying out, she bit down on her lip. Fear tightened her protesting muscles. She heard someone stir behind her, but she didn't take her eyes off the scene unfolding in front of her.

The other car's door opened, and a man stepped out. He was older—early fifties, at a guess—with dark hair and a build much like Sam's. He came around to stand in the beams of light, his hand outstretched in welcome.

Sam took it, and the two talked for several minutes. Then both men turned to face the parked cruiser. Marly couldn't sit still another minute. As she slid from the car, she peered over the back seat. Chris had fallen asleep, but Emma was gazing at her with worried eyes. She lifted Matt's gun so that Emma could see it.

Butterflies crawled over Marly's stomach lining as she walked toward the men. Something pestered the back of her mind. A thought. An idea. It wavered there, just out of reach.

Her fingers went to the pocket of her skirt for the soothing comfort of Matt's nine-millimeter semiautomatic. Emma had pulled it from the gun cabinet and handed it to Marly right before they went out the window.

"Marly, this is Captain George Brent," Sam said, gesturing toward the other man.

"So, this is Matt's wife," the newcomer growled by way of greeting.

Her stomach lurched. His voice sounded so familiar, yet she was sure she had never met the man before.

"Ex-wife," she corrected. She pretended not to see his extended hand. All her instincts screamed in alarm. She was suddenly very conscious of the heavy weight of the small gun in her pocket. It was an effort to keep her hand from reaching inside to touch it.

The captain's eyes were too close together. They studied her as though fascinated by what they saw.

"I knew your husband," he said. "Fine officer."

The butterflies morphed into something larger, more frightening.

"I'll get Chris and we'll go," Sam said.

"Go where?" The words came out more sharply than she'd intended. Something was wrong here. She could feel it. Something in the way Sam's friend watched her.

"Take it easy," George said in his rumbling voice. "There's nothing to worry about. You're not under arrest, Ms. Kramer. We're not even going to the police station. Not just yet, anyhow. We'll go back to my place. I'll call a couple of people I know, and everything will be fine."

"Marly?" Sam had reached the cruiser's door, but he stopped, frowning at her.

Chris popped his head up from the back seat. "Sam?" Fear strained his voice, which carried clearly to where she stood.

"Ah, the boy," George murmured.

Fear pierced her as the niggle was released and thoughts tumbled over themselves faster than the speed of light. Her hand moved toward her pocket.

This was what they had overlooked. Internal affairs had been investigating five men, not four. The captain had also had access to the evidence room. Sam had said George restored old cars for a hobby. He was married. She had even spoken to him on the phone right after Matt was killed. He was the captain Matt had been working undercover for.

"My God." Her words were a whisper of sound. She saw his eyes harden, heard Sam trying to reassure Chris.

"It's okay, Chris," Sam said. "That's George, my friend."

She took a step back, hardly breathing. Her fingers delved inside the pocket of her skirt for the weapon.

"No, Sam. He's the one. The one from the park."

The shrill words penetrated her brain even as Sam yelled, "Marly, get down!"

But it was too late. She had twisted to run, but large hands clamped on her arm, biting into her flesh. Marly kicked and struggled, but George pulled her back against his chest as though she weighed nothing at all. His grip was unbreakable. He thrust the barrel of his gun up and under her jaw. She never had a chance to bring her hand from the pocket where her fingers clenched around the butt of Matt's small gun.

"Hold still," George snarled, squeezing her so tight he cut off her oxygen. Marly stopped moving. "Come away from the car, Joe, or she's dead."

Sam had dropped down beside the open car door. She saw his gun poking over the top of the window. "You know better, George."

Sam's voice was utterly calm. Marly swallowed back the bile that threatened to choke her. His tone soothed her. She couldn't cave in to panic. She couldn't think about the gun under her chin or the fact that her instincts had been correct. She inched her hand out of the pocket, just enough for Sam to hopefully see what she held.

"I'm not kidding, Joe."

"Neither am I. We both know how this is going to work."

"No." The word was a growl, low in his throat. "Put the gun down now."

"I can't do that. The minute I do, you'll shoot me and then her and then Chris."

Marly knew Sam was right. George Brent intended to kill all of them. Her biggest fear was that Sam *would* set his gun down before she was in a position to use hers. Tension radiated off George.

"Let her go, George."

"You know better."

"Why?" Sam demanded. "Why Porterfield and Ray-back? It doesn't make sense."

"Don't waste any sympathy on Porterfield. He was on the take, can you believe it? I knew, but I couldn't prove it. IA suggested a sting operation, so I recommended Matt for the role of Rayback."

The arms coiled around her body tightened fractionally. George was wound so tight he could explode. Marly was petrified that he would squeeze the trigger by accident. Or that she would.

"Why?" Sam asked again.

"So I could kill him, of course. He was sleeping with my wife." Anguish and bitter passion made him secure his hold on her even further.

"She left me. For him!" George shook with outrage. "Matt didn't care about her. He screwed any woman he could get into bed. Cassandra was too blind to see that. She wouldn't come back, even when I begged her."

His gun shifted, dropping lower, to her neck, but the arm around her body didn't loosen. Marly swallowed hard, waiting for an opening.

"I decided to frame Porterfield. You can understand, Joe. That way I got rid of a dirty cop and that fornicating bastard all at the same time. You know how I feel about dirty cops."

"Yeah, George, I know."

"It would have worked, too. When I caught him going through your locker in the gym, he was planting evidence on you. Isn't that a laugh? I was going to frame him and he was going to frame you."

George chuckled—a harsh, ugly sound. His breath smelled fetid. It reeked of stale whiskey and fear. Marly tried to still the trembling that threatened to overwhelm her.

"I was sorry it had to be you. You're a damn fine cop, Joe, but it was too good an opening to miss. Porterfield didn't know I'd seen him stash the money. He was sweating bullets as we stood there and chatted. I really wanted to tie it all to him, but—" George shrugged "—he left your locker open."

"So you removed the money, planted it at my place and switched guns with me."

"Damn it! You shouldn't have stopped in the park that night, Joe. I could still have pinned it on Porterfield if you hadn't showed up. I was going to put your gun and the money in his car after I killed Matt. His prints would have been on your locker, and they would have traced the gun in your holster to impound. We could have nailed him."

George squeezed her, but Marly knew he wasn't even aware of her anymore. This was between George and Sam. He'd moved the gun a little lower. She could no longer feel it against her skin. She needed a distraction so that he'd loosen his hold a bit more. Once she threw herself clear, Sam would have a shot—or she would.

"Instead you're going to kill three more innocent people, is that it, George? What kind of a dirty cop does that make you?"

"Damn it, Joe, I have no choice. The kid was there that night. When I finally figured out who he was, I had Porterfield send him to her boys' camp. It was perfect, don't you see?"

"Yeah, I see. You were going to kill a young kid, and frame me for that murder, as well."

George clicked his teeth together with an audible sound. "I had to get rid of all the players. Porterfield met me right on schedule, but you showed up before I could get to the boy. Then you got Marly here to alibi you." He squeezed her, none too gently. "That was a boon I hadn't expected. We've got a pretty good case now. Everyone is convinced you killed her ex for personal reasons. Too bad you didn't die in that car crash I arranged."

His grip relaxed marginally.

"How did you know Sam would get in my car?" Marly asked in a quiet voice. She held the gun firmly, concealed by the folds of her skirt.

"Sam? Oh, you mean Joe." George chuckled. "The car accident wasn't intended for Joe," he said with a sneer. "I merely wanted to be sure you wouldn't be around to connect me to Matt. Darling Cassandra called your house that day, trying to warn him about me. And I couldn't be sure what she'd said to you."

His hold loosened just a bit. He was focused on Sam, not on her. The weapon was still a threat, but maybe, if she was quick and fast...

"The woman caller," Marly said slowly. "I didn't even know who she was."

"But I couldn't take that chance, now, could I?"

"Did you kill her, too?" Sam asked.

"What do you think?" His voice changed. Almost a plea for understanding. "I didn't mean to, but I heard her on the phone, trying to find Kramer to warn him. I started hitting her, and I just couldn't seem to stop. You know, Marly, if you'd been a better wife to Matt, maybe none of this would have happened."

Marly brought her heel back against his shin, surprising him. She almost jerked free, but George was snake-quick, yanking her into shield position again before she could tear free or use the weapon in her hand.

"Don't you dare blame me," she snarled at him. "My husband was a jerk."

"Shut up," George growled, nearly snapping her neck as his arm constricted. "Now come out, Joe. We need to end this."

"Nope. It's not gonna happen that way."

"Stand up, or I'm going to pull this trigger."

"You won't do that, George, because if you hurt Marly, *nothing* will stop me from killing you."

"Then we'll do it the hard way." He marched Marly forward, his arm still firm across her chest. "I'm sorry, Joe. I didn't want it to end like this."

If he got within range, he would shoot Sam. She couldn't let that happen. Marly glanced down and saw the black top of his shoe. If she could get a clear shot at his foot...

George propelled her toward the police car. Without warning, Marly let her body sag. George was pulled off balance by her sudden shift in weight. The passenger door on the police car abruptly opened, and a shot reverberated against the night sky.

Marly saw her target and pulled the trigger. Her shot went straight into George's foot. He roared in pain. His gun discharged in a stream of flame even as Sam sprinted forward.

Marly twisted free and turned, bringing her weapon up, but Sam was already there. Sam brought his gun arm down in a savage arc, and George tumbled to the asphalt, his weapon skittering across the ground.

Sam towered over him, breathing hard. His rage was so intense, his gun hand trembled. Marly bent to retrieve the weapon George had dropped.

"Sam?"

"You were supposed to let me rescue you," he told her.

There was a ringing in her ears. Probably from all the gunshots.

"Sorry." Her voice shook just the tiniest bit. "You were taking too long."

"Yeah? Well, Emma had to climb over the seat. The back doors on the cruisers don't open from the inside. I was trying to stall until she could get in position."

"An' she got stuck," Chris piped up from a few feet away. "I had to push."

George groaned. In the distance there was the sound of a siren. Sam shook his head as though to clear it.

"Emma radioed for backup," he said weakly.

"Of course, she did. Are you okay?"

Sam looked down, a strange expression on his face. There was something dark and wet on his gun hand.

"I think I hurt my hand when I hit him."

Marly darted forward as he began to sway. Her eyes found the small, neat hole in the arm of his shirt.

"Chris, tell Emma to call for an ambulance, then get over here. Sam's hurt." The panic in her voice communicated itself. Chris fled across the parking lot. Sam swayed, and she grabbed for him.

"Damn it, cowboy! Don't you dare pass out on me."

"Wouldn't think of it, boss," he told her as he collapsed on the tarmac next to George.

Chapter Thirteen

"Hi, Lee! How's our patient today?"

Lee Garvey looked up from the chair at the foot of the hospital bed and gave Marly a cocky grin. "Not bad. Only one nurse quit, the aide threw a bedpan at him, and the candy striper refuses to work on this floor until he's discharged. I'd say he's definitely on the mend."

"Shut up," Sam snarled, rubbing at his sore arm where the bullet had created an unwanted path through his body.

Marly tied a cluster of balloons to the foot of his bed and moved forward. A smile softened her lips. She dropped a paper sack to the floor and leaned over so that he had a clear view down the sexy blue silk blouse she wore. Marly wasn't wearing a bra. Before his mind could do any more with that, her lips fused with his in a deeply satisfying kiss.

Her face was flushed and her eyes were half-closed when she pulled away, her crystal earrings sparkling in the fluorescent lighting.

"You're raising my temperature," he warned her. "My nurse won't like that."

"Then maybe I should take you home."

Sam pushed back the sheet. "I'm ready."

"So I see."

Lee cleared his throat and looked up at the ceiling. "Why do I get the feeling I'm superfluous?"

Sam didn't lift his eyes from Marly. "Because you are. Go catch a bad guy or something."

"And here I came all the way over here to visit with my good buddy and tell him about Duncan."

Marly pulled free so that Sam turned his disgruntled attention back to Lee. "What about Duncan?"

"Marly agreed to prosecute, providing they give Carter immunity for testifying against him. That should take care of Duncan's days behind a badge."

"And George?" Marly asked.

"His attorneys are looking into an insanity plea. I don't think they'll have much trouble there—he's nearly catatonic now."

"It was George who trashed your apartment, wasn't it?" Sam asked quietly.

"Yeah. He planted some money and that auto repair book, even though IA had already been through my place. I think killing his wife sent him over the edge."

"He was a good cop once," Sam stated.

"I know."

Marly reached for Sam's hand. "I brought you something."

He nodded toward the balloons, grateful for the change of topic. "So I see."

"Nope. They're outside. Come on in, guys!" she called out.

Emma pushed open the door, and the room erupted the type of noisy burst that can only come from a group of children. Marly perched on the side of the bed with a satisfied grin as Sam found himself surrounded by six exuberant boys.

"Can I see the bullet hole?" Mickey asked.

"No, dummy," Hector argued, giving him a shove. "It's just a scar by now."

Mickey shoved him back. "Well, then, I want to see the scar."

Emma separated the two with a caring hand on each shoulder. Marly exchanged grins with Sam as Jerome walked around the bed to stand beside him. "I got somethin' for you," he said.

With his good hand, Sam accepted the crude soap carving of a small boat. He had to swallow a couple of times before he could trust his voice to come out even. He didn't dare look at Marly. "That's terrific, Jerome. You're really improving."

"Yeah." He snuck a brash grin in Marly's direction. "I told you I could do better with *my* knife. When your arm gets better, I want you to show me how to carve real wood, okay?"

"Deal."

"I got you this," Chris told him, edging his way to the front position on the other side of the bed. "It's my lucky rabbit's foot." He dangled the small white object from its chain. "I figure you need it more than I do. You probably used up all your luck getting shot again."

Sam glanced at the sudden earnest expressions on the faces of all six children. Again, he had to swallow past the lump in his throat. "It was only a flesh wound, Chris," he managed to say.

"It nicked an artery," Marly reminded him.

"Yeah. There was blood everywhere," Chris told him. "Just like before when you got shot in the head."

"Thanks for reminding me," Sam muttered.

"You coulda bled to death," Hector added, with an eleven-year-old's relish for gore.

"But I didn't. I'm fine."

Marly caught his eye. "Oh, you're better than that, cowboy. Much better," she whispered.

Zeke shyly proffered a much-fingered envelope before Sam could retort. "My mom sent you this letter. She don't write too good, but she wanted to thank you for taking care of me."

"Mine, too," Hector put in, handing him another note.

Chris frowned. "So when are you comin' back?"

"Yeah, Sam," Donald agreed. "You're supposed to take us riding, remember?"

Marly smiled. "Better give him a few more days to recoup, guys. He'll need to take slow, quiet rides first."

Sam leaned back, feeling better than he had in days at the subtle double entendre he heard behind her words. "Slow and quiet, huh?"

"Very slow," she agreed, with a hint of mischief that heated his blood.

"You're going to take him home with you?" Lee cut in. "Do you think that's wise?"

"Yes," Emma stated, with such conviction that Lee blinked.

Marly chuckled. "Probably not. The man causes me no end of trouble, but I'll need a foreman now that I've fired Carter. Even one with an allergy to hay is better than none."

This time it was Lee who grinned. "You're never gonna live that one down, Joe. A Texan who's allergic to hay. Ha! I'm not allergic to hay," he told Marly slyly. "You could dump this clown for me. What do you say?"

"I'd say you're asking for a black eye," Sam warned, but his words were drowned out by the children.

"Can you ride?" Hector demanded of Lee.

"Do you know how to whittle?" Zeke wanted to know.

"Uh, well…"

"We'd rather have Sam," Donald stated.

Mickey nodded. "Yeah, he knows how to do all kinds of cool things."

Marly laughed, and Sam squeezed her hand.

Lee tilted his chair back on two legs. "Okay, I know when I'm licked. What about your job status, Joe?"

"I tendered my resignation with the police department yesterday."

The chair came down with a thump. "Why? You've been exonerated. You're in line for George's job."

Sam watched Marly. "I've had a better offer."

Lee looked from one face to another. "I hope you two aren't going to do anything stupid, like ruin a good relationship by getting married."

"You're gettin' married, Sam?" Chris asked.

"Good," Emma stated. Her plump face was wreathed in a smile.

"Can we come?" Zeke wanted to know.

"Yeah," Donald added. "I like wedding cake."

Marly began to laugh. "He hasn't asked me, guys."

Jerome frowned thoughtfully. "I think you should, Sam. Marly's okay, for a girl."

The boys began to chatter, and Sam rubbed the palm of Marly's hand suggestively with his thumb. "Oh, I'm gonna ask her, but when I do, it will be done right, with flowers, candlelight, champagne—"

"You, on bended knee?"

His eyes gleamed at the devilment in hers. "Don't push your luck."

Lee laughed. "I want pictures. I could make a fortune at the station house."

"Forget it," Sam growled, wishing everyone would take the hint and disappear.

"Are you asking me, Sam?"

The room seemed to vanish as his gaze focused on the love he could read so clearly in her expression. "Yeah, I'm asking, Marly. I love you."

Her smile lit the room. "I thought you might, but it's always nice to hear the words."

"He's allergic to hay," Lee reminded Marly.

"Well, I'm sure I'll find another use for him."

"She has a sassy mouth," Sam told his friend.

Emma beamed.

"He can whittle," Jerome offered.

"Thanks, pal. The truth is, I discovered I like working with the kids, Lee. I'm going to look into getting certified. There's even a chance we can get Marly's program reinstated, and if not, there's always Utah."

Lee looked affronted. "You'd be willing to move, Marly?"

She regarded Sam with amused tolerance. "Given the right incentive."

"I'll see what I can do about that," he promised. "First, we'll see what we can do to finesse the situation here. Meantime, I'm going to take a part-time job with that security company that came sniffing around last month. Marly can train horses, and I'll train business executives about white-collar criminals."

"No, we want you to come back to the farm with us," Chris demanded.

Hector frowned. "Yeah, Sam, it won't be fun without you."

Sam leaned over and ruffled his hair. "Oh, I'll be there, fellows. Unless Marly says no when I ask her to marry me."

"I will make the wedding cake," Emma announced.

"Chocolate," Zeke insisted. "You make good chocolate cake. Doesn't she, Marly?"

"Marly won't say no, Sam. Will you, Marly?" Chris demanded.

Marly didn't reply. She released Sam's hand and reached for the sack on the floor. Sam held his breath as she regarded the sea of watchful faces around her. "Looks like there'd be a lynching if I said no."

He released the breath and grinned in sheer relief.

From inside the paper sack, Marly withdrew his battered black Stetson, a pile of clothing, and a pair of scuffed cowboy boots. "Here, guys. Make yourselves useful. Emma and I will check Sam out of here. Then we're going to take this cowboy home."

"The doctor may have something to say about that," Sam warned her. But he didn't really care what the doctor had to say. He was more than willing to go anywhere, anytime, with this woman.

"Don't worry, I already got you sprung. He released you into my custody...with a large sigh of relief, I might add."

"Yeah? He didn't say a word to me about getting out of here."

"You were too busy growling at him to give him an opening. Besides, I asked him not to. I wanted to surprise you."

Sam leaned back, feeling better than he ever had. "You always manage to do that."

She winked and started for the door. The kids began to squabble over who got to hold Sam's hat until he was ready to put it on.

Lee raised his eyebrows. "Hey, you aren't going to leave me here alone with them, are you? Aren't you going to stay and help him get dressed?"

"Nope. I get the fun part." There was love and laughter shining from her eyes as she paused in the doorway to slant Sam a wicked smile. "I'm going to help him take everything back off as soon as I get him home. This is one cowboy who isn't going to die with his boots on."

HARLEQUIN®

I N T R I G U E®

COMING NEXT MONTH

#405 HERO FOR HIRE by Laura Kenner
Lawman
When seasoned P.I. Will Riggs was hired by a suspicious attorney to test his fiancé's fidelity, Will knew Sara Hardaway would pass with flying colors. Trouble was, when Will started falling for the woman he'd been hired to seduce, *her* fiancé suddenly and mysteriously wound up dead....

#406 THE VALENTINE HOSTAGE by Dawn Stewardson
Eyewitness
Monique LaRoquette was testifying against sexy Ben DeCarlo, a man she'd seen commit murder, when he grabbed her in the courtroom—and escaped! Alone with her kidnapper, Monique's heart started playing tricks. Was love blind—or were her lying eyes mistaken about Ben after all?

#407 FOR YOUR EYES ONLY by Rebecca York
43 Light St.
Nothing could stop Jenny Larkin from searching for her friend's murderer—not even her blindness. But all too soon she could feel someone watching her, taste fear enveloping her. There was only one man who could help her—but Jenny would never let Ben Brisco back into her life, no matter what the cost....

#408 FEVER RISING by Maggie Ferguson
Deep in the heart of Chicago Memorial, a deadly virus rages—and Dr. Jeffrey Knight has run out of possible cures. He has only one hope—Raven Delaney, his former love, the one connection between all the victims. Their passion blazes again as the fever burns...but then Jeff, too, falls ill. In time they're sure they'll find the killer... but will they find the cure?

AVAILABLE THIS MONTH:

Look us up on-line at: http://www.romance.net

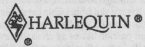

FREE VALENTINE'S BROOCH! $9.95 U.S. retail value

This Valentine's Day Harlequin brings you all the essentials—romance, chocolate and jewelry—in:

VALENTINE *Delights*

Matchmaking chocolate-shop owner Papa Valentine dispenses sinful desserts, mouth-watering chocolates...and advice to the lovelorn, in this collection of three delightfully romantic stories by Meryl Sawyer, Kate Hoffmann and Gina Wilkins.

As our special Valentine's Day gift to you, each copy of *Valentine Delights* will have a beautiful, filigreed, heart-shaped brooch attached to the cover.

Make this your most delicious Valentine's Day ever with *Valentine Delights!*

Available in February wherever Harlequin books are sold.

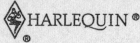

◆ HARLEQUIN ®

Harlequin and Silhouette celebrate
Black History Month with seven terrific titles,
featuring the all-new *Fever Rising*
by Maggie Ferguson
(Harlequin Intrigue #408) and
A Family Wedding by Angela Benson
(Silhouette Special Edition #1085)!

Also available are:
Looks Are Deceiving by Maggie Ferguson
Crime of Passion by Maggie Ferguson
Adam and Eva by Sandra Kitt
Unforgivable by Joyce McGill
Blood Sympathy by Reginald Hill

On sale in January at your favorite
Harlequin and Silhouette retail outlet.

HARLEQUIN®

I N T R I G U E ®

In steamy New Orleans, three women witnessed the same crime, testified against the same man and were then swept into the Witness Protection Program. But now, there's new evidence. These three women are about to come out of hiding—and find both danger and desire....

eye WITNESS

Start your new year right with all the books in the exciting EYEWITNESS miniseries:

Don't miss these three books—or miss out on all the passion and drama of the crime of the century!

Look us up on-line at: http://www.romance.net   EYE1